"I'm here for my challenge."

Wyatt's gaze flickered down her as if assessing her once more and wondering if he'd gone crazy asking her back. The distrust was there as clear as day. Determination sprang through her like a runner out of the starting blocks. Amanda hiked a brow when he said nothing, deciding a little challenge of her own was in order.

"I guess I am, too," he drawled in a voice she bet jurors found almost hypnotizing in a courtroom.

She had to give him credit, though; his tone was civil for the first time since she'd met him. They could build on that.

"I promise you won't be sorry. I'll get results."

"I'll make sure you do."

His words were meant as a warning, but they made her smile widen. "I think we are going to have some fun, Mr. Turner."

Books by Debra Clopton

Love Inspired

*The Trouble with
   Lacy Brown
*And Baby Makes Five
*No Place Like Home
*Dream a Little Dream
*Meeting Her Match
*Operation: Married
   by Christmas
*Next Door Daddy
*Her Baby Dreams

*The Cowboy Takes a Bride
*Texas Ranger Dad
*Small-Town Brides
   "A Mule Hollow Match"
*His Cowgirl Bride
**Her Forever Cowboy
**Cowboy For Keeps

*Mule Hollow
**Men of Mule Hollow

DEBRA CLOPTON

was a 2004 Golden Heart finalist in the inspirational category, a 2006 Inspirational Readers' Choice Award winner, a 2007 Golden Quill award winner and a finalist for the 2007 American Christian Fiction Writers Book of the Year Award. She praises the Lord each time someone votes for one of her books, and takes it as an affirmation that she is exactly where God wants her to be.

Debra is a hopeless romantic and loves to create stories with lively heroines and the strong heroes who fall in love with them. But most important, she loves showing her characters living their faith, seeking God's will in their lives one day at a time. Her goal is to give her readers an entertaining story that will make them smile, hopefully laugh and always feel God's goodness as they read her books. She has found the perfect home for her stories writing for the Love Inspired line and still has to pinch herself just to see if she really is awake and living her dream.

When she isn't writing, she enjoys taking road trips, reading and spending time with her two sons, Chase and Kris. She loves hearing from readers and can be reached through her Web site, www.debraclopton.com, or by mail at P.O. Box 1125, Madisonville, Texas 77864.

Cowboy For Keeps
Debra Clopton

**Steeple
Hill®**

Published by Steeple Hill Books™

STEEPLE HILL BOOKS

Steeple Hill®

Recycling programs for this product may not exist in your area.

ISBN-13: 978-0-373-81481-7

COWBOY FOR KEEPS

Printed in U.S.A.

And Jesus answered and said unto him,
If a man love me, he will keep my words.
—*John* 14:23

This book is dedicated to Chuck Parks. My life changed the day God sent you to my front door—what a wonderful beginning that blind date turned out to be! I love you, Chuck…you are my very own God-loving, honorable *cowboy for keeps* :)

Chapter One

"Are you sure this is what you want to do? I just can't believe it."

Amanda Hathaway met her boss's sympathetic, if somewhat startled, gaze. It wasn't what she wanted, it was her only option. "Yes. It is, Joyce. I've given it a lot of thought and I want—I *need*—to move strictly to adult cases." Adults, not children. Not the kids she'd loved working with—felt called to work with.

"But you've always loved working with children," Joyce Canton said as if reading her mind. "And you have such a gift. Don't you want to think this through?"

Amanda took a deep breath, her chest constricted with the strain she was feeling. "I have, Joyce. This is not easy for me. But I don't have the heart for it anymore."

"I can't believe that."

"Being around…" The words trailed off because she couldn't voice the words that being around children right now made her feel ill. What good would she do as a physical therapist when she couldn't look at her patients without crying or feeling hollow? "It's tearing me up inside" was all she could manage. She had to change her life. And she had to do it now.

"He was a jerk, Amanda."

Joyce's words emerged in a growl of disgust, one completely the opposite of her normally professional demeanor. Amanda blinked hard as her eyes began to burn. She looked away, willing herself to keep her composure. God had a plan. He did; she just didn't understand it. And that didn't make what she was feeling any less heartbreaking.

"You can't let what *he* said and did have this kind of power over you," Joyce continued. "If I were a man I'd go over there and I'd punch him."

Any other time Amanda might have smiled at her boss's show of affection, but today she just couldn't summon one. Her fiancé—no, her *ex*-fiancé's decision ate at her. "He only expressed his true feelings," she managed, willing herself to truly understand him. Anger wasn't going to help her in this situation. Anger very seldom did help, but in this instance it would simply exaggerate her already shot emotions. "He can't be faulted for being honest."

"Honest. *Honest!* The man knew the facts and asked you to marry him. Then out of the blue he drops this bomb on you. How could he ask you to marry him and then break it off because you can't—"

Joyce didn't finish the sentence as her voice broke. Her eyes welled with tears. She snatched a tissue from the box on the desk and dabbed her eyes. Amanda had experienced the same anger and disbelief when Jonathan had made his revelation three endless weeks ago. But then, reality sank in and she knew that deep down she'd been expecting the breakup all along. And how could she blame him? How could anyone blame a man for realizing he couldn't marry a woman who was unable to give him children? She couldn't, and that was where the anger had dispelled. She was twenty-four years old with no hope of ever carrying a child. Her chest constricted again.

She still wasn't sure why she'd started dating Jonathan in the first place. She'd told herself she wouldn't date. Not dating held less risk for her. But then, Jonathan had asked her out for lunch—and when she'd said no, he'd kept coming back. She'd finally agreed. She revealed the cold hard facts of her situation to him on their second date. She hadn't expected to hear from him after that, but he'd assured her that her infertility didn't matter to him. After a whirlwind few weeks, he'd told her he loved her and said adopting children would be totally fine with him. Deep down in her heart, Amanda had known there would be few men in the world who would take on marrying a woman who'd not only lost the ability to carry children, but who had also lost a leg. *Two strikes against you,* the tiny voice in her head chanted. That voice was not good and she knew it, but it wouldn't hush.

"He lied to you, Amanda. What kind of man would do that?"

Focusing on the reality of the situation, Amanda shook her head. "He probably was being honest with himself." Amanda knew it was true. "He made the right choice for himself…and for that I'm grateful—otherwise it would have been wrong for me in the end, too. And besides, you and I both know I rushed into this."

"I really can't believe you are defending him. Although I do agree that it was a rushed relationship. I think you were settling if you ask me. He came along and asked and you jumped at the chance."

Amanda felt a twinge of agreement with that statement. Was that what she'd done? "I learned a long time ago that there are some things you have no control over. That God is in control of our lives and he has a plan." She just hadn't expected it to hurt so much—after all, she'd already faced this reality once in her life at the age of fourteen when the doctors had explained to her that they'd had to give her a complete hysterectomy while they repaired all the internal damage she'd sustained in the accident that had almost killed her. She was blessed to be alive and she'd thought she'd come to peace about her life and her circumstance. But she'd been wrong. After Jonathan ended their relationship, her emotions had spiraled into a tailspin. She'd been struggling for the last month to cope—not sleeping and turning down each job Amanda had offered her.

It didn't make sense. She had a full life. Her career as a physical therapist specializing in children's needs had been borne from that accident. Because she knew she couldn't have children of her own and because she'd had to be fitted with a prosthetic leg at such a young age, she'd been drawn to help kids.

She was good with children, especially those in need of prosthetics. She understood how they felt, and could relate to the many emotions they experienced because of the loss of a limb.

And it made her feel good because she had also been an inspiration to them when they realized life hadn't ended. She'd helped them see that their dreams could still become reality wearing an artificial limb.

That wasn't true for her anymore. Coming face-to-face with Jonathan's choice, she'd also realized that she'd been living a lie.

She couldn't have children of her own. She could never know what it felt like to feel that tiny, precious life growing inside of her. Suddenly it was unbearable.

With shaking fingers Amanda slid the folder of what was supposed to be her new assignment across the desk. "I want—" she paused, digging deep "—I *need* to move to adult cases only."

Amanda couldn't withstand the sympathy in Joyce's gaze any longer. Pushing out of the chair, she moved to stand beside the large window overlooking the busy streets of San Antonio. The thunderstorm that had been hanging over the city all morning had finally given in and was raging full force. She could relate as a violent streak of lightning flashed across the sky. An explosion of thunder immediately followed. She took a shaky breath and reminded herself that she'd overcome so much in her life. She'd thought she'd had it all under control. What a lie that had been. "Jenny told me she had to back out of that long-term job in the hill country. The one with the man in the plane crash."

Joyce didn't look pleased. "She did, but you don't want that. It's—" Joyce stopped speaking and sank into her seat behind her desk as Amanda turned from the window. "It's a tiny town almost a hundred miles from any town of any real size. You don't want to go there—"

But she did. "That's exactly what I want." She felt ill but knew this was what she had to do.

"No, it isn't. This is a three-month on-site assignment. You don't—"

"I do." She moved to stand across the desk from her boss. How could she make Joyce understand that she was trapped in a dark hole and the idea of this job seemed like a crack of light showing her the way of escape? A lifeline had been revealed. "I have to do this job. It's exactly what I need."

"But," Joyce started. They held gazes for a long moment and Amanda was almost certain that Joyce could see into Amanda's damaged heart.

"Give me the chance," she urged her. "You know I can do the job."

Another long moment passed. "They want someone with more experience."

"I have enough experience."

"You know…" Joyce murmured thoughtfully as she tapped her fingers on her chair arm. "You actually might be perfect for this job. The other brothers said they thought their brother was depressed. You could help with that. You know about that journey."

Yes, she did. It was what she was fighting off from happening to her again. This job gave Amanda a ray of hope. Her heart kicked up and the constriction eased when Joyce reached for a file on the top of the stack on her desk. A file labeled *Wyatt Turner.*

"I was going to have to turn this job down because Jenny couldn't do it. You know how I hate to pass up jobs. But are you sure this is what you want? I'm comfortable with the idea of you doing the job. I just want to know your state of mind is okay."

The very idea of spending three months in a tiny town away from everything was what Amanda needed. Her eyes hurt with unshed tears of relief. "I'm sure." She hadn't been able to pray since Jonathan broke off their engagement, but she found herself praying now that she would get to do this job.

"Wyatt Turner is a man of means," Joyce said at last. "He can afford to hire a full-time PT to help him all day if he chooses, and so he's doing it. You will be coming up with not only his daily therapy, but also helping out with other things he might need—acting as his personal assistant or cooking if he wants you to. It's an odd job, but the pay is excellent and I promised his two brothers that I'd find the perfect person or I would turn the job down."

"No need for that. It sounds wonderful—"

Joyce held up a hand. "Not so fast. The brothers said Wyatt is impatient with his injuries and will probably not be the easiest person to work with. Being a high achiever and fairly powerful man in his own right, he'll probably be demanding. Are you absolutely certain you can handle this job?"

"I can handle it."

"Why don't you take his file and read over it carefully before you commit to this?"

Amanda didn't need to look over the file. She knew she was capable of getting this man back on his feet. He might be demanding and he might take her for granted. But she could help him and he would help her by getting her away from San Antonio.

"I can do this job." She met Joyce's gaze with determined eyes.

Joyce studied her hard, clearly weighing

the decision on all sides. "Then it's yours," she said at last. "I'll let Wyatt's brothers know you'll be there on Monday."

Amanda's heart clamored with the first real excitement she'd felt since Jonathan's words had slammed a hole in it. "Thank you," she managed.

"Honey, I'm praying while you're there you'll realize that none of what Jonathan said is true."

Amanda knew it wasn't that easy to fix the emptiness that filled her. It was far more than Jonathan's words that were affecting her. It was as if they'd released long-dormant emotions she hadn't been able to experience as a young girl when she'd been told there were no children of her own in her future. Her being so young, the loss of a leg had been more devastating than the nebulous idea of being barren. But it was different when a man told a grown woman he couldn't marry her because he wanted children she couldn't give him. It had opened a wound she hadn't realized was there.

She pushed that thought aside and focused on the positive moment now. "I just need to get away and get my head on straight," she said, but she was afraid even that wouldn't fix the emptiness and the loss that now gripped her heart fresh and new. "Please don't worry. I can do this job."

"Then it's yours. I hear Mule Hollow, Texas, is a lovely little town even if it is off the beaten path. You do realize what town this is?"

With memories and intentions tangling in her mind, she hadn't even given the name of the town any consideration. Now she shook her head.

"It's the one that advertised for women to come marry their lonesome cowboys a couple of years ago," Joyce said. "There are cowboys, new wives and babies there now, from what I can find out. But you should know that Mr. Turner's ranch is located several miles away, so you may not be that involved in anything going on in town."

"I can handle it." Amanda needed air and room to breathe and think. "I'll be fine." She didn't want to think about anything right now, not the heartache that was eating at her over her life or the losses she'd suffered. Or Jonathan. She just needed to get away and focus on work. And maybe somewhere during that time this utter sense of emptiness and worthlessness would loosen its hold around her heart.

Maybe in that small town, on that big ranch and in that open space she could find her footing again.

Wyatt Turner shot his brothers, Cole and Seth, a scowl. "It's my body that's broken, not my mind." The wheelchair he'd been sentenced to for the next few weeks felt like cement blocks chained around his waist. Three weeks ago he'd awakened in the hospital lucky to be alive—especially with both legs still attached. Ever since that moment, he'd been fighting to find some kind of balance with the anger he was feeling.

Four days ago he'd been flown in by helicopter to the ranch he and his brothers owned, and he'd been mothered and worried over by his brothers, their wives and the ladies of Mule Hollow—who'd decided that food was the answer to his problems—to the point that he was about sick. He loved them all, but enough was enough. He just wanted to be left alone.

Needed to be alone.

Because of this, his brothers were getting the brunt of his bad temper.

A month ago he'd had the world by its tail. He'd had everything in control. He'd managed to match his younger brothers up with good wives and he'd been able to rest easy that he'd done his parents proud in his family responsibilities. His brothers were happy and that had made him happy. But then he'd crashed his plane and turned his world upside down. The stupidity of his actions ate at him as much as the consequences did.

Looking at him with the patience of Job, his middle brother, Seth, spoke up. "We aren't so sure your mind is working. The fun-loving brother we know and enjoy is sitting in this dark house looking like he hasn't showered in days."

"Seth—" Wyatt bit the word out but Cole, his youngest brother, butted in.

"We love you, bro, and you know you have to snap out of this. You're not going to be in that chair for long."

"Look, you two, go to work and leave me alone. I'm not joking." He had lost his sense of humor three weeks ago.

Cole held up his hands and gave a lopsided grin that usually made anyone and everyone smile along with him. "We're goin'," he said. "No call to get so riled up. That temper's one of the reasons we're worried about you."

Wyatt hiked a brow as a shooting pain ripped through his left hip and tore through his lower spine. He gripped the arm of the wheelchair with his hands and willed his expression to remain pain-free. "I'm only skimming the surface here," he said, trying not to clench his teeth. "You need to stop worrying about me. I'm an adult." Who'd made a bad error in judgment.

"Cole, let's give him some space." Seth headed toward the door. "But Wyatt, whatever you do, don't run Amanda Hathaway off. Yes, you want to be alone, but remember you need her. And the agency said she was the perfect person for the job."

"Yeah, so give her a chance," Cole drawled. "Don't forget Mule Hollow is a long way from the nearest rehab center. It wasn't easy to find a physical therapist willing to come all the way out here to live for three months."

"*And* you can't do therapy on your own,"

Seth added somberly. "Not this time. Not even you, Wyatt."

He got that loud and clear.

"As stubborn as you are," Cole prompted when Wyatt remained silent, "and as driven, there is no doubt in our minds that you'll be back up globe-trotting in record time. With the right physical therapy program. So stop worrying—and we know you are. You can't hide it from us. Just like you can't hide the fact that you're in a heap of pain right now."

"I'm fine," Wyatt snapped as his gut tightened at the denial as the spasm began to ease up a bit. They came and went at their leisure and he'd begun to wonder if this was what a woman felt like when she went into labor…if so, it was a miracle there were children born. "Look," he said. "I don't need you two knuckleheads trying to run my life—"

"*Oh, man,* you did *not* just say that!" Cole hooted, his eyes dancing as he stared at Wyatt in disbelief. "You, the master of interference—"

"Not that the two of us are complaining," Seth interjected with a grin. "You found us both our wives and we are eternally grateful. But you aren't yourself these days, Wyatt.

Not since the accident. We've got to help you get out of this funk you're in from being out of control of everything."

Seth's somber, determined gaze locked with Wyatt's. He knew Seth couldn't be budged when he had that look—it was chock-full of Turner stubbornness. It was true he was in a "funk," but it was only to be expected. He was letting down his clients and his firm because he'd been careless…and careless was unacceptable in his book.

"I should have gone back to Dallas so y'all wouldn't worry—"

"No, you shouldn't have," Seth countered emphatically. "We love you and want what's best for you. Therapy out here on the land you love is the best way to get you healed up."

"That's all we care about," Cole added, all laughter and teasing gone. That in itself told Wyatt how concerned they were for him. "You just need someone to help you get the full range of movement back into that hip and arm. Then you'll be your old overachieving self again. If it were either one of us in your position, this is what you'd be doing for us and you know it."

It was true. He'd have meddled in their lives until he got what was best for them. "I'll be fine," he grunted, not liking losing control of his life like he had. It was not a feeling he'd ever experienced before, and he wasn't dealing well.

"Yeah, you will be after the PT arrives. *Now* we'll go to work." Seth walked out the door.

Cole sauntered after him, but stopped in the doorway. "Hang tough, big bro."

Through the window, Wyatt watched them leave. Their boots thumped loudly as they hurried across the rough wooden porch and down the two steps to the old stone sidewalk that led to where they'd parked the ranch truck earlier. He reminded himself that his little brothers were only looking out for him because they loved him. Still, having the control taken away from him fisted him up inside. Giving control of his life over to anyone wasn't something he did...but it seemed he had no choice. If he wanted his life back he was going to have to trust this Amanda Hathaway.

Seth and Cole wouldn't have hired someone who wasn't capable, he assured himself an hour later as a red SUV pulled over the cattle guard.

Feeling suffocated inside, he'd moved his wheelchair out onto the porch. He waited as a woman got out of the vehicle. She was young, about twenty. No, she'd have to be around twenty-four or -five to have a degree in physical therapy *and* have any kind of experience at all. They'd said she was good at her job…hard to believe if she was as young as he suspected.

She seemed ill at ease as she tucked a strand of fine brown hair behind her ear and looked his way. Being ill at ease didn't give him any more confidence in her than her young age.

Wyatt's eyes narrowed as she walked up the path. Surely this wasn't the woman he was supposed to put his confidence in? If he was going to have someone living on the premises for the next two or three months, invading his privacy and telling him what to do, he expected someone who looked as if they could do the job they were hired to do. His ire escalated with each step she took toward him.

She was medium height with a slight

build—no way could she help him get in and out of the wheelchair. She came to a halt at the foot of the steps. Up close it was worse. She had the fresh face of a kid, made more so by the splash of freckles and large doe eyes that looked up at him with what he could only call fear. *Seth and Cole were dead meat!*

"Who are you?" he demanded before she had time to say anything.

"I—well, I'm Amanda. Amanda Hathaway."

This was a joke. It had to be. He was notorious for pulling jokes on his brothers. This would be just like the two of them to get him back for stunts he'd pulled. But he knew it wasn't true. Even they wouldn't pull a stunt like this now.

Nope. This was the woman he was supposed to give control over to—the woman he was supposed to trust with his future.

He didn't think so.

Despite what his little brothers thought, he could still make decisions on his own and that started with telling Amanda Hathaway she wasn't staying.

Chapter Two

Wyatt Turner didn't look right in the wheelchair.

It was the first thought that had hit Amanda when she'd spotted him sitting on the porch. Her confidence had faltered as she'd driven the three hours to Mule Hollow—not surprising since she hadn't been feeling like herself. Seeing Mr. Turner did nothing to help matters.

He was an extremely physically fit man with a broad chest and the lean build of someone used to working out. A man who took care of himself—though she'd already assumed that about him. Joyce had said he was a high achiever, driven to be the best. If that was true, keeping physically fit would fit the profile.

He was handsome—or would be if he didn't look so angry. He had black, wavy hair and bold features including a strong jaw, which at the moment was dark with a five o'clock shadow. It wasn't, however, his look and build that had her smoothing her hand across her flyaway brown hair in a display of nerves. No, it was his eyes. Hard, intense cobalt-blue, they narrowed and grew cold as they studied her. These were the all-seeing eyes of a man who read people for a living.

He probably hid his thoughts well. He looked as if he only let a person, or a jury, see what he chose to let them see.

Amanda stilled her nerves. She didn't have to look close to see he was not happy to be in a wheelchair. He was probably not used to needing someone else.

Despite her resolve that she could handle this job, Amanda's heart fluttered with worry and she wondered if she'd made a mistake in coming.

No mistake.

This man's intensity might serve to be her saving grace. If he was as demanding as she assumed he would be, that meant all her time would be consumed.

And all-consuming was exactly what she needed right now.

"I'm sorry I'm running a bit late. I'd hoped to be here before lunch but traffic on I-35 was killer."

"How old are you?"

His question caught her off guard, halting her rambling. "I'm twenty-four."

"How long have you been a physical therapist?"

Okay, so he had a right to know these things. But still, he hadn't even said hello. "Two years. I graduated high school early and started college two years early. I have experience, Mr. Turner, if that's what you're worried about." The realization that he might not have wanted her here hit her.

"You graduated two years early?"

She heard the astonishment in his voice.

"How did that happen?"

"I had an accident and almost died when I was fourteen. I wasn't able to attend class." It shouldn't have been any big deal, but the fact that he had yet to be cordial at all set everything on end. She assumed he was going to make her stand in the sun until he was satisfied with her answers. She lifted her chin, shifted her weight to her good leg and smiled. "I was hit by a drunk driver. I was training to be a cross-country runner on the freshman cross-country team and was out running near our house. I... Like I said, I nearly died. My parents homeschooled me after that. It was work-at-my-own-pace. I decided I liked to move quickly."

She saw the flicker of surprise in his dark eyes—good, she'd meant to get a reaction out of him. He knew about nearly dying and surely would relate to that. It was easy to see he was spoiling for a fight. Anger wasn't uncommon in his situation. She suspected he was probably stunned to find out that he wasn't invincible. Overachievers often thought they were untouchable. That they had everything under control and nothing could go wrong. She had news for him—it happened to the best of them. Including herself.

Life was not controllable. At least not completely.

"Look, I'm sorry, but this isn't going to work."

"What do you mean this isn't going to work?" Surely he didn't mean what she thought he meant.

His face hardened more—if that were even possible—and his jaw jutted. "Just what I said, Ms. Hathaway. My brothers and your employers all knew I expected a fully capable, highly trained physical therapist for this job. I'm sorry you've been brought all the way out here, but I don't have the luxury of time and can't waste what I do have."

"Mr. Turner, I might be young, but I'm capable of doing this job. I wouldn't have come if I hadn't been. You've read my résumé, I'm sure."

"Actually, no. My brothers handled these arrangements."

"Well, then, you also should know that the majority of my work has been done with children and teens. But that doesn't discredit me from being qualified to handle your case." Nor did her lack of a leg, but obviously his brothers had chosen not to tell him that, and they must have had their reasons, so she didn't say anything.

"That doesn't change anything." His expression was blank. "I'll make sure you're paid for your time coming out here. This is not going to work."

Amanda watched in shock as he pressed

the forward button on his wheelchair with the fingers of the arm not in a sling and guided it toward the open doorway.

"The agency I work for doesn't have another therapist open for this job." She hoped something would change his mind; obviously it wouldn't be anything about herself that would do it. "Being all the way out here is going to cause a big problem when it comes to finding a good therapist. I'm good. Are you sure you don't want to reconsider?" She hadn't expected that she'd get turned away.

He halted at the door and shot her a glare— that look took her faltering thoughts from stunned disbelief to complete peevishness! *The man is really being unreasonable.* Of course she had no clue what was going on in his head, she reminded herself. For all she knew, he might be like this all the time. Boy, would that be an unpleasant way to go through life. However, looking at him, something told her he wasn't. Something told her he was struggling. And she saw pain in his eyes right then, even as she watched him. He winced slightly, favoring his left side where she knew his hip and lower back injury needed her attention.

"I'm sure," he said, his words almost a grunt, but he held on and almost covered up the fact that he was having a spasm.

Even in pain he was stubborn, though Amanda had no doubt about his sincerity. She could see that changing his mind wasn't something he did. She knew from his profile that he was probably also used to getting his own way, doing things his way and more than likely able to buy anything he needed in order to make it happen. This could very well be doomed from the start—begging him to keep her on was not an option that would work for either of them, no matter how much she wanted to stay.

"Then I guess that does it." Disheartened in so many ways, she fought to think rationally—something she'd been having a bit of a problem with lately. Her stomach decided to step in and help her out by letting out a long, drawn-out roar. It broke the uncomfortable silence that stretched between her and Wyatt. That was one way to end their meeting: food. It might help her refocus. She'd been stuck in traffic and running late, so she hadn't taken time to stop for lunch. "Is there somewhere in town I can get a bite to eat?" she asked, fighting to keep her tone neutral.

He'd entered the house and turned the chair—probably so that he could slam the door in her face! His brows locked in consternation as he stared at her through the screen. For a minute she wondered if he'd expected her to beg him for the job. She needed this job to take her mind off her own troubles, but she would never beg. He had to realize he needed her. Surely he knew how badly his injuries needed attention before they began to worsen. That would start to happen while he looked for someone to replace her. Time was of the essence, she wanted to say—but he was a smart man and he knew this.

"Sam's is the only diner in town. You can't miss it."

She held his gaze and almost challenged him...any other time she might have, but not today. "Thanks," she said, turning to go. She'd eat and then she'd call Joyce. If anyone was going to fix this it would be up to her boss. With her back held straight she retraced her steps to her vehicle. In her heart of hearts she hoped Wyatt would reconsider and stop her before she drove away...but she knew he wouldn't.

Wyatt Turner was not a man who changed his mind. He also wasn't the only person who was good at reading people. It was a trait she'd learned after the accident, watching nurses and doctors and her parents when they gave her hard information. It had come in handy in her profession as she evaluated her clients' needs and signs of pain.

It was a shame that it did her absolutely no good now…then again, maybe she wasn't as good at it as she'd thought she was. She'd read Jonathan about as wrong as possible.

Or maybe she really hadn't. Maybe she'd only imagined in their relationship what she'd wanted to see there.

She got into her car, pulled the strap of the seat belt securely about her and stole a glance toward the house. He was watching her…and he was rubbing his hip since he thought she wasn't looking. So be it. She started the SUV and drove away. She watched the house disappear in her rearview mirror and felt more lost than she had in ages. What was she going to do?

The feelings she'd been able to set aside as she'd headed toward this job crowded back in around her.

In the early days, working with kids gave her something to focus on other than herself. Now she didn't even have that comfort any longer. God had a plan for her life. She clung to that belief, but right now it was giving her little comfort.

Turning onto the blacktop, her thoughts turned to Wyatt Turner and she found herself wondering if that was how he felt. If so, he had her sympathy. Even if he had just fired her.

Wyatt needed out of this wheelchair.

He needed out before he went crazy. It had to happen and it had to happen sooner rather than later.

It *would* happen—he'd make it happen as quick as possible. Something about Amanda Hathaway bothered him. She would only have slowed down his progress.

Letting her go had been his only option. Still, he hadn't liked doing what he'd done.

She wasn't up for the job, it was obvious. It niggled at him that he'd judged her by her appearance, but he didn't have time to go soft. He hadn't gotten where he was in life by going soft. The facts were that she wasn't strong enough—she was small and young.

There was no way she'd be able to handle strenuous training like he expected and needed. And she'd worked with children! Of all things. What had Cole and Seth been thinking?

They'd wanted to remind him about how important his physical therapy was and yet they'd gone and pulled a sorry stunt like this.

His doctors had assured him he could make a full recovery, but only with hard, diligent work. There wasn't an ounce of quit in him—never had been, but this physical disablement had thrown his world upside down. Every time his hip and back seized up he felt weak…if he let his guard down. If he didn't work absolutely as hard as he was supposed to there was a chance he would always have a limp and lower back pain.

He'd admit that deep inside he was scared. If he let up, if he messed up in the least little bit he wouldn't come out of this as strong and healthy as he'd been before he'd botched things up with his stupid error in judgment when he'd decided to fly his plane in unsafe conditions.

That was the scariest thing—how weak he felt. As if to show him who was boss, pain shot through his left hip once more and attacked his lower back with a vengeance. This time it was so strong he groaned before he could stop it. Perspiration beaded across his forehead as he grimaced against the pain. He closed his eyes, he counted to ten, willing his muscles to relax. Tensing up made the spasm worse—not a good thing.

Sucking in a heavy breath, he tried to relax and let the pain pass. *What if I can't make it back to the way I was?* The question sliced through him like a knife to a wound.

It had been three endless weeks since he'd crash-landed his twin engine plane in a pasture during a storm. It had happened not long after he'd left Mule Hollow and was headed back to Dallas. He'd taken time he didn't have to fly home to congratulate Cole on his wedding engagement. Since he was responsible for matching up Cole and Susan, he'd wanted to make the quick day trip and share in the joy of the moment. If he'd listened to his gut—which was usually right—and stayed the night, taken time to really enjoy the moment with them, he'd have been all right. But enjoying the moment wasn't something he did. Instead he'd rushed off in the middle of dangerous winds and a severe thunderstorm. He'd been arrogant enough to believe he could handle the storm. What an inane bit of stupidity.

When had he decided he could control everything?

He hadn't closed the door after watching Amanda drive away and now he stared across the land that had been in his family for over a hundred and fifty years. It was in this place his roots ran deep and was from his ancestors' example that he'd become the man he was.

Being used to control was a good thing, he reminded himself. It had driven him to where he was in his career as an attorney. It would get him through this. Taking another deep breath, he began to relax as his mind cleared and the pain began to recede.

Good blood ran through his veins. Hard-working, upstanding—well, upstanding except for his good ole great-great-great-great-great-grandpa Oakley—him being upstanding was questionable. By and large the Turner men and women were tough. Generations past had stared across this land that stagecoaches had crossed on their way to this old stagecoach stop. Like this house, his ancestors had stood the test of time and so would he.

His brothers had been right in bringing him home.

This place had always been good for his soul.

Two months. He would get better and he'd get to work. He would not let himself get waylaid by debilitating, unproductive thoughts again. He hadn't been feeling like doing anything except sitting in this chair and feeling sorry for himself. It wasn't something he understood or wanted, but that was what had been happening. He wasn't sleeping and his attitude stank. But lately he hadn't been able to do anything about it. Cole and Seth had known and they'd taken action when he wouldn't. Their action had helped him—jolted him enough to fight…and fight was what he needed.

Action: that was what he needed.

He needed a therapist capable of helping him achieve his goal. The soft, sweet-faced Amanda Hathaway hadn't been up for the challenge.

Still, even he couldn't help admiring the way she'd walked away with her head held high.

Chapter Three

As dismal as Amanda felt, the sight of Mule Hollow perked her up the instant it peeked over the horizon. Why, it was darling! So cute with its bright stores, welcoming flowerpots along plank sidewalks and window boxes. Driving down Main Street, she began to smile. It was a wonderful feeling.

There was a pink two-story hair salon called Heavenly Inspirations, a bright yellow feed store with peacock-blue trim, a real estate office painted A&M maroon—which she was a big fan of—and beside it was Sam's Diner painted a bright grass-green.

Amanda pulled into the parking space and got out. More stores just as brightly painted stood all along Main Street. The dress store and candy store across the street were memorable as well as the community center a few doors down the wooden sidewalk. She watched a cowboy clomp into the feed store down the way and felt very nostalgic. She half expected to see a horse tied to a hitching post. This was smiletown if ever there was one. Just lovely.

There was a really huge older home that anchored the town at one end. It had a green roof with turrets on each corner and a sign that read Adela's Apartments. Amanda studied the structure with interest. What would it be like to just walk in there and rent an apartment? Start over?

Crazy. She was thinking crazy and she knew it. It had been one thing to pretend she was running away from her life when she was coming here for a job, but this—this was simply a daydream, and it was too much. She was not the kind of person who ran away. At least not for good. She would get her head on straight. She would.

Yet it was as if Wyatt Turner's stormy scowl had burned its way into her head.

She wondered if he'd slammed the door after she left. Something about the man intrigued her, despite his easy dismissal of her.

Maybe it was simply that she hated to see anyone in pain. Maybe it wasn't the man himself that kept her attention but the fact that she knew she could help him.

She could help him if he'd only give her the chance.

The man had to want her help. There was no getting around that. She couldn't force anyone to accept her. Especially a man like him! She bit her lip and stared at the rooster weather vane sitting on the top of one of Adela's turrets. No seesawing or riding the fence for him. Jonathan came to mind and she cringed. Jonathan had probably known his mind long before he'd finally spoken it. Maybe if he'd have cut her loose early like Wyatt had she wouldn't be hurting so much right now.

At least Wyatt had been honest with how he felt. For that she admired him—even if he *did* need her.

A squeaking door sounded behind her. "Norma Sue, are you or are you not going to come out tonight and see my moon lily?" a woman said.

"I told you I would, but you were too busy running your mouth in there to hear me."

Amanda turned. Two women were coming

out of the diner. They looked up from their conversation and stopped short when they spotted her.

"Hello there," the one who'd just been accused of running her mouth said. She had bright red hair and was wearing a daffodil-yellow capri set.

"Hello," Amanda said.

"Honey, you look a bit dazed. Are you all right?" the woman called Norma Sue asked. She was a robust, strong-looking woman with wiry gray curls and a big wide smile that spread all the way across her face. "Being dazed is understandable when folks first look at all these wild colors. It tends to make people's heads spin."

"Now, Norma Sue, we don't know that this is her first time to see Mule Hollow—"

"Esther Mae." Norma Sue stared in disbelief at her friend. "Have you ever seen her before?"

"Well, no—" The redhead looked at Amanda sheepishly.

"Then there you go. She's as new to Mule Hollow as that calf I had born this morning." She directed her hazel eyes back at Amanda.

"Tell *her* this is your first time to our little metropolis, isn't it?"

Amanda smiled, liking these two on the spot. "First time."

"See, I knew it was!"

"I'm Amanda Hathaway." She held up her right hand like she was swearing in at court and said, "And yes, I am new in town and I love it. I was just admiring the colors."

Both ladies grinned as she let her hand fall.

"It does attract folks—kind of like red flowers attract hummingbirds. I'm Esther Mae Wilcox, by the way, and this is Norma Sue Jenkins." She leaned forward slightly as if telling a secret. "She's my sidekick."

"Ha! Don't believe a word of it," Norma Sue huffed. "She's *my* sidekick."

It was easy to visualize these two getting into all kinds of trouble.

"What brings you to town?" Esther Mae asked. "Are you here looking for a cowboy?"

The statement took Amanda by surprise, even though she knew the background of the town. She said the first thing that came to mind. "I don't know, do you have some for sale?"

"We don't sale 'um, but we sure do give

them away at the altar," Esther Mae volleyed back.

"To the right women," Norma Sue added. "You need one, don't you? I don't see a ring on your hand."

Amanda glanced at her finger where three weeks earlier there had been a ring. She blinked hard and stilled the sudden rolling of her stomach.

"Honey, you okay?" Esther Mae asked.

"Y-yes, I'm fine." Meeting two sets of curious eyes, she pushed the jab of pain back into the corner of her heart where she'd barricaded it. "Um, how exactly do you get these cowboys to the altar?" she asked, a little too brightly. A vivid picture of Norma Sue behind them with a shotgun popped into her mind. "And is it legal?"

That got her chuckles from both women.

Norma Sue's grin was wide. "Oh, the preacher makes it legal and the cowboys usually go willingly after a spell. Ain't that right, Esther Mae?"

Esther Mae was watching her intently and Amanda feared she might have seen more than she'd needed anyone to see.

"Esther Mae, did you hear me?"

"Of course I did," she said, her cinnamon brows puckered above alert green eyes. "So are you really telling us you haven't heard about us?"

"No, I was teasing. I've heard a little about Mule Hollow." It hit her that she had been teasing—it seemed like forever since she'd done that. She glanced at her ring finger, as empty as her heart felt. As her life was now. And yet she'd just teased these ladies spontaneously.

It was a good sign that maybe the entire trip out here hadn't been a waste. "And no, I'm not looking to marry one of your cowboys. I came here from San Antonio for a job I was supposed to start today."

"A *job?*" Esther Mae cooed. "What job?"

Amanda's stomach growled loudly, reminding her why she'd come to town. She slapped a hand over it.

"Whoa, girl, that's not good." Norma Sue grabbed her by the arm. "C'mon, Esther Mae, we've got to get this young'un inside the diner and fill that stomach up with some of Sam's good cooking."

Esther Mae scooted to the door. "While you

eat, you can tell us what job brought you to our neck of the woods."

And just like that Amanda found herself being escorted into the diner by her new best buds. One thing was certain, this trip had been anything but boring. She might be headed home in an hour, but today—though disappointing in that she'd been dismissed basically on sight—she felt better.

"So you know about our little advertisements for wives?" Norma Sue asked.

"Yes, I don't think many people, at least here in Texas, haven't heard about it. My boss reminded me. I had forgotten about it when I first got my assignment, but I read a few of Molly Jacob's columns back when they started." Molly was a local newspaper reporter who'd begun writing a column about the goings-on of the little town that advertised for wives and it had been syndicated across the country. She enjoyed reading, but the column had taken a backseat to her always-full work schedule, training for the marathons she loved to run and…then, the connection she'd finally found with Jonathan. As soon as the thoughts of him came she pushed them away, refusing to go there.

"Then you know gals like you come from all over to marry our men. See, look over there." Norma Sue pointed across the diner to a table where four cowboys were hunched over plates of food.

Esther Mae had slid into a booth and patted the seat beside her. "We've married off over a dozen couples with several engagements pending right now. And babies are arriving now, too. It is so exciting."

Amanda sat down and inhaled the scent of food wafting through the air.

"Our church is busier than one of those tacky Las Vegas drive-through chapels." Norma Sue grunted as she took the seat across from her. "Of course we just lost our preacher so we've got to find a new one to carry on the ceremonies."

"Oh, *brother,* you two again!" A little man came out from the kitchen and headed to their booth. "I can't get rid of you gals no matter how hard I try." He settled teasing eyes on Amanda. "Hangin' out with these two'll get you inta trouble, little lady. Just so you know." He held out his hand. "I'm Sam. Welcome to my place. These two git my Adela into more trouble than you can shake a stick at."

Amanda introduced herself as she grabbed his hand and gave a firm squeeze, nowhere *near* the iron grip he attacked her with, but still, she gave as good as she could.

He grinned. "Fer a tiny woman, that's some shake ya got thar."

She flexed her hand. "You aren't so bad yourself. My daddy always did say a person's heart was measured by the firmness of their handshake. You must have a giant heart."

That won her a big grin; his weathered face creased with a mischievous look. "Ain't nobody 'sposed to know about my big heart. So let's keep that one quiet. If these two or a couple of others, who shall remain nameless at the moment, were ta suspect I had a big heart, they'd thank I was a pushover and then I wouldn't never be able to get my bluff in on 'em."

Norma Sue rolled her eyes. "Don't believe none of it. If it wasn't for me and Esther Mae and his two 'nameless friends' keeping him in line, the man would be bored out of his brain."

"Ha! I wish," he grunted. "So, what brangs you ta Mule Hollow? And why in the world are you brangin' these two back into my establishment when I jest got rid of them?"

Amanda laughed—it felt good. "Honestly, Sam, I just met them outside and they dragged me in here—"

As they all chuckled with her she thought they reminded her of her cantankerous grandparents who lived on a farm in West Texas.

"We thought she was here looking for a cowboy," Esther Mae told Sam. "We were just telling her about what nice ones we have around here."

Norma Sue nodded toward the window. "There are two of our success stories about to come through the door right now. That taller one is Seth Turner. He got married a couple of months ago. The other one is his younger brother, Cole. Cole is having a wedding in about four weeks—had to be put off because his big brother got injured in a plane crash."

The door swung open and the men burst inside like cowboys looking for trouble. Instantly she saw the resemblance to their brother. Their expressions were serious as they scanned the room, but nowhere near the intensity of Wyatt's.

Esther Mae nudged Amanda in the ribs. "Those two Turner men are handsome, but you should see that big brother of theirs!"

"He's something worth seein', all right," Norma Sue whispered, leaning forward over the table.

She didn't have to be told that these were the brothers who'd hired her. They'd stopped just inside the door and their searching gazes locked on to her almost instantly.

Norma Sue looked from them to Amanda as the cowboys advanced toward them. "Hey, boys," she drawled. "Y'all look like you're lookin' for somebody."

Both men swept their Stetsons from their heads. The taller one with the more serious eyes that reminded Amanda of Wyatt's tugged at his collar. "Are you Amanda Hathaway?"

Amanda nodded as suddenly all eyes turned on her.

"We've come to apologize and ask you to reconsider."

"Seth, what in the world do you want Amanda to reconsider?" Esther Mae asked.

Norma Sue's eyes widened. "*You're* Wyatt's new physical therapist! Aren't you? The one that was arriving this morning?"

"Of course," Esther Mae snapped. "I don't know what I was thinking."

"Was," Amanda corrected. "He fired me on the spot." She cringed, not having meant to blurt it out that way.

"No, he did not," Esther Mae gasped.

"I'm afraid so," Amanda said, more evenly. "So unless he changes his mind, I'll be leaving after I eat. I can't help anyone who doesn't want me to." It was true. But as she looked around at the faces of her new friends, her heart tugged and she wished things had worked out differently.

"I'll be." Sam rubbed his jaw. "Ain't this here a bunch of interestin' information."

"It sure is," Norma Sue drawled. "What you boys got to say about this?" she said at the two men who'd been patiently standing by.

"First, we should introduce ourselves. I'm Cole and this is my brother Seth. We have most definitely come to hire you back. The ball's in your court, just name your price."

"Well," Esther Mae harrumphed. "This is getting better by the moment."

Amanda hadn't expected this, but it didn't matter. She shook her head. "Like I said, I can't help someone who doesn't even want to give me a chance. Believe me, it won't work for me and it won't work for your brother."

"He's not against you," Seth said. "He's got a lot on his plate. Don't get me wrong, he's going to be a bear to work with, but he needs you and he knows it now."

"What do you say?" Cole asked, giving her a wink and a lopsided grin.

They were cute and they obviously cared a lot about their brother. But that still wouldn't make this work. There was only one thing that might. "The only way I'd take the job back is if Wyatt asked me himself."

"That-a-girl." Sam chuckled. "Hold your own. When my Adela gets back home from her sister's, she's gonna want to hear all about this."

"That's what he thought." Seth reached into his shirt pocket and pulled out a folded piece of paper. "I think this should do it." He handed a yellow paper to her.

She eyed the page as she took it. It was from a yellow legal pad, and when Amanda opened it there was one sentence scrawled in a bold masculine print across the middle of the page.

If you are up for the challenge, come back and prove it. Wyatt Turner.

Her lip twitched and she held back a smile. No way had she expected an apology. What really startled her was that he'd written exactly what she'd needed…a challenge. She and Wyatt Turner needed the same thing.

Folding the paper again, she looked at the brothers. Giving them an encouraging smile, she took a settling breath. "Okay. I'll stay. I need to eat and then I'll head back out there. Will you please tell your brother that I said I was up for the challenge. But—*is he?*"

Chapter Four

He was waiting on the porch when Amanda got out of her car. In some ways he reminded her of George Strait with his dark hair and square chin. And despite the intensity of his eyes, she thought there was a hint of mischievousness lurking there as he watched her walk up the path. In doing her job, no matter what personal crisis she had going on in her own life, she must be positive and figure out the best way to bring her patient around. Not just physically but also emotionally—she had to be positive and engaging in a way he would respond to.

Somewhere in the background a cow mooed—well, several cows mooed, sounding as if they were heralding her arrival. She halted in front of Wyatt and gave him her best grin. "I'm here for my challenge." His gaze flickered down her as if assessing her once more and wondering if he'd gone crazy asking her back. The distrust was there as clear as day. Determination sprang through her like a runner out of the starting blocks. She hiked a brow when he said nothing, deciding a little challenge of her own was in order.

"I guess I am, too," he drawled in a voice she bet jurors found almost hypnotizing in a courtroom.

She had to give him credit, though: his tone was civil for the first time since she'd met him. They could build on that.

"I promise you won't be sorry. I'll get results."

"I'll make sure you do."

His words were meant as a warning, but they made her smile widen. "I think we are going to have some fun, Mr. Turner."

The scowl of earlier returned. "I'm not interested in fun. I want out of this chair and on my own two feet and I want it yesterday."

She chuckled—not a good thing but unstoppable. He was actually very cute in his state of *irked.* "Then you shall be. *Will* and *want* work together to make things happen. I can just look at you and know you're going to push your limits every time I ask you to do an exercise. So for now, put your scowl away and relax. I promise you, it's going to be all right." She sounded like she was talking to one of her kids. Not dissimilar— teens were just as anxious to be up and about as Wyatt. His impatience was nothing new to her and that was a good thing.

"I know with the pain you're in you might be worrying whether you'll ever return to your normal lifestyle. Stop worrying, you'll be back if you do as I ask."

"You always this sure of yourself?"

"In this case, *your* case, yes, I am." Their gazes held and she wanted so badly to tell him again not to worry. But she saw the skepticism alive and well in that look.

She wouldn't say more for now. He'd think she was patronizing him if she kept on. She'd been watching him for pain and didn't think it was too bad at the moment, but it was there. With a strained back, cracked hip, along with the tendon and ligature trauma his hip had gone through, the spasms would come and go with a vengeance. Not to mention the constant pain from the damage to his shoulder. She could help with all of that.

Later. "So I guess I'll put my things up and get settled. Seth and Cole told me the temporary trailer was set up and ready for me. Is it out back somewhere?"

"By the barn. I'll show you," he said, his words clipped.

"That would be great." She turned and headed back to her car, not even considering telling him that she could find it on her own. The last thing he needed was to be treated like he was helpless. There was a ramp that had been built off the side of the old porch and the ground was level all about the house. That top-of-the-line motorized wheelchair would have no trouble maneuvering the landscape. The man exuded energy, even in a wheelchair. It was a miracle that he was alive, though. During the small-engine airplane crash he'd pulled and stressed nearly every muscle, tendon and ligature on the left side of his body. Even the fact that he had no broken bones other than a hairline crack in his hip was yet another miracle. She suspected surviving sitting still on a porch might kill him, though. She completely understood how he was feeling.

Running with the rising sun was more her style. She wondered if he'd run in the mornings prior to the crash. She had a feeling he was a runner, too. One who liked to run outside. Then again, he might be a treadmill runner—too white-collar to run outside...not that that was a bad thing. She just preferred to do her running outside.

"Did you bring much?"

"I have a car full of things. Not all luggage, though." She laughed. "Most of it I'll be setting up in the therapy room. But all I want now are my suitcases." They'd made it to the SUV and he waited, watching her as she opened the glass window and then lowered the tailgate of the SUV. For some reason his watchful eyes made her self-conscious. She tucked her hair behind her ears before she reached for the first suitcase and hefted it to the ground.

Without speaking, he reached with his good arm and took some of the weight from her by grabbing the bottom of the case. "Thanks," she said, knowing that every little thing he did that was positive would help him move forward.

"You're welcome," he said as she grabbed the slightly smaller one. He helped with that one, too. She'd loaded it all up herself and was quite capable of removing all the luggage herself but still she appreciated the fact that Wyatt Turner was—behind his poor manners earlier—a gentleman. This was instinctive on his part. She wondered if his mother had drilled the manners into him as he grew up.

"You're looking at me like I've surprised you," he said as she shut the tailgate.

Grinning, she stepped out of the way as she lifted it. The movement brought her closer to him than she'd been. "I guess I'm a bit shocked you're a gentleman," she answered truthfully. *He'd asked.*

His lip actually twitched! "My mom would have skinned me and my brothers alive if we weren't."

Bingo. "I thought so."

"You're thinking, otherwise I wouldn't be?"

"It crossed my mind when you booted me off your property," she said drily. "And that was after I'd driven three hours to get here—

with no lunch!" She looked at him ruefully as she extended the pull arm of the large suitcase and set the overnight bag on top of the big one, fastening them together for transport.

His eyes crinkled around the edges. "I'd apologize—"

"*But...*" she drawled slowly. "You wouldn't mean it." She knew it was true.

"I did what I thought best at the time."

"That's exactly what I thought you did. And that's why I'm just teasing you." She winked at him, picked up the smallest suitcase with the hand on the same side as her prosthetic. The action balanced out the weight as she grabbed the handle of the other case and started rolling it behind her across the lawn.

The thing about Wyatt was exactly that— he did what he thought he needed to do. After Seth and Cole had left the diner to return her message to Wyatt, the ladies had told her that he'd pulled out all the stops when it came to finding wives for his two brothers. He'd seen women he thought fit them and made certain they came in contact with each other. It was really sweet! The man was a romantic—who would have thunk it?

It did her broken heart good to know there were men like him in the world looking out for those they loved. It was a very admirable quality in a man. But even if she hadn't known all of that, she'd already figured out that he was an honorable man just by the way his brothers talked about him.

"You could roll that second one," he said, driving up beside her. "Or better yet I could carry it."

She glanced at him. "You don't need to carry it. You're absolutely right—I could roll it if I wanted to."

"But you won't."

"I wouldn't get any kind of workout from rolling it, and besides—" She'd almost said it helped her keep her balance. Instead she said, "I'd be a bit of a hypocrite if I harp on my patients about keeping their strength and agility up and I wasn't practicing it myself."

"True," he mused.

They walked around the old homestead in silence. The large travel trailer came into view and the size startled her.

It was sitting out under a giant oak tree, not far from the low-slung barn. It was huge compared to some she stayed in while on-site. But then again, looking at Wyatt, she wouldn't put it past the man to have had a double-wide mobile home sitting back here for her. There was just something about him—even if she hadn't read his profile and didn't know that the man was worth a bundle—she'd still have the feeling that only the best was good enough for those around him.

"I hope this will do," he said. "Cole and Seth assured me that your boss said a small one was all you needed."

"I don't call this small. Believe me, this is more than enough." She smiled. "I'll feel like a queen in there compared to the tiny place I had on the last job. Don't get me wrong, though, it was great. It was one of those little round jobs that had only room for a bed, a small television and a table for my books. I have to admit taking a shower in a three by three space also occupied by the sink and toilet was a bit of a chore, though."

He looked aghast. "How long did you do that?"

"Six weeks. I wish it had been longer, but the insurance ran out…" She'd hated leaving. Shawn, the teen, needed more help with his new prosthesis. She was still in contact with him, checking on his progress—or at least she had been until three weeks ago. Joyce was checking on him now and told her he was getting along pretty well, doing everything she'd instructed him to do. She had confidence that he would be fine. He was a totally determined teenager. Just like she'd been. It was the younger kids she'd worried the most about. They needed services longer to acclimate to their pros-thetics and she'd hoped—at least she had before she'd walked away—that someday she could do something to help them more. Now she wasn't sure if she could ever go back to working with young patients.

"You obviously like what you do to put up with that sort of thing that long."

Wyatt's words broke into the wandering thoughts. "Oh, I *love* my job." Even now, moving from children to adults, she did love it. "Not many people can say they are blessed to be where they are in life. I can. Tiny shower stalls and all." She didn't add that she'd had to give up the part that she'd once loved the most. No one needed to know that, and that fact still didn't change her love of her profession. It just altered her reality.

His expression grew troubled. "I know what you mean," he said, almost under his breath as he looked away, out toward the pastures that stretched from the barn endlessly. Two football-goal-size lines formed between his brows, and his expression darkened. That scowl told her she'd somehow just shot down the little progress they'd just made. The man had actually lightened up for a few moments. It was a glimpse, but nonetheless a start.

Deciding that for now she'd said enough, she opened the door to the trailer and stepped up on the single step. "Thank you for this." She'd wondered what was roaming around in his head. Something was troubling Wyatt. Maybe it was worry about his injuries. Maybe something more. Helping him with his pain and getting him up and about would help him physically. And mentally, too. "I'll unpack and get settled. Is there anything you need me to do this evening? I could give you a therapeutic massage to help with that pain." Therapist plus general factotum was an odd arrangement for her but she was looking forward to it.

He didn't look at her. "No, we'll get everything figured out tomorrow." Unsmiling, he drove his wheelchair back toward the house without further elaboration.

Watching him, Amanda felt his pain. Still, she knew he was going to be all right physically with time.

She wondered if he realized that. He'd almost lost his life in that plane crash. There might be more going on in his head than anyone realized. She said a prayer for him as he rounded the corner and disappeared.

He'd seemed all alone in that moment. As alone as she was. *Don't let your thoughts go there.* Right. She was here to work, and to get her mind off her own troubles. The last thing she needed to do was empathize so strongly with her client that she let it bring her down. He was counting on her and she wouldn't fail him.

Glancing about the land that surrounded her, she breathed deeply. It was hot and dry, the reports of drought were increasing and the cool wind that had suddenly started blowing in across the dry grass was a pleasant surprise. Tomorrow she would run and gain every feel-good endorphin that running would give her.

Tomorrow she would begin to prove to Wyatt that he'd been right to hire her.

She realized that she wanted to make him smile—just as she always did her kids. A real smile. Not just a twitch of his lips, but a full-out smile.

And she would. The thought energized her and it gave her yet another purpose for being here.

Tomorrow *would* be a good day.

Bam! Bam-bam-bam.

Amanda woke with a jolt as the entire trailer shuddered. She sat up in bed, glanced at the alarm clock. It was four in the morning and something was ramming her house! *Bam!* It started over. The entire travel trailer shook like she'd just been hit by a earthquake. Scrambling for her yellow flowered housecoat, she yanked it on then glanced out the window above the bed. In the moonlight she saw…hogs?!

Hogs! She was surrounded by wild boars with long, ugly tusks. *"Fifteen,"* she gasped, counting the animals. They were every-where. Big ones and small ones and every size in between. What was she supposed to do? Did she need to try and wake Wyatt?

She slipped on her sock and then pulled her leg on in a movement that had become as natural as standing. Heading to the door, she peered out the window. There was a light on inside the house. Was Wyatt up? Did he know these animals were out here? Another slammed into the trailer, making her cringe at the thought of dents. Nibbling her lip, she tried to figure out what she needed to do. The porch light came on and she wasn't sure how that would help since Wyatt was in a wheelchair, but at least she wasn't alone out here anymore. Maybe he would call his brothers.

Reaching for her warm-up pants, she pulled them on, not exactly sure what she expected to do. She heard someone yell something. She swung back the curtain and saw Wyatt driving his chair out onto the back porch. No! What was he thinking? Her shoe was already on her prosthetic, so she quickly put on her other one and reached for the doorknob. Wyatt was now at the edge of the porch and it was easy to see even from this distance that he was not happy.

Her heart was pounding and her temper soared. The hard-headed, injured man was outside with a herd of wild hogs!

Didn't wild hogs tear people up with their horrible tusks? A vivid memory of *Old Yeller* came to mind. The man had lost his ever-lovin' mind and was going to get himself hurt if she didn't do something. Surely he would go back inside.

Nope. Not him. She was fumbling for the door as she watched, in horror, him drive his chair right to the edge of the porch—what she remotely planned to do was a mystery to her. She couldn't just let her patient get mowed over by a bunch of hogs, though.

"Wyatt," she called through the cracked door. "What are you doing?" This was something that was completely off the chart on what she'd ever been prepared to handle.

"*Close* that door, Amanda."

His command cracked through the night like thunder, sending the hogs scattering in a wild frenzy of movement. And of all the rotten luck, one big, giant shadow headed straight for Wyatt!

Amanda flung open the door and stepped to the ground. "Run," she screamed, taking a step and realizing she couldn't move fast enough because of the ruts the animals had plowed into the ground—

"Get back!" Wyatt yelled at the top of his lungs just as the animal veered away from him and—to her great relief—raced toward open pasture.

Amanda's heart thundered.

"What were you thinking coming out of that trailer?" Wyatt demanded, his eyes glittering in the moonlight. "Do you know what those animals can do to you?"

"Me! *Me!*" Amanda would have flown across the land between them, she was so hot, but had to settle for making slow progress to keep steady. It was amazing, the small amount of time the hogs had been there, how destructive they'd been with their rooting. Mounds of dirt and holes turned the land into a hazard. Because her prosthetic was stiff, a misstep on uneven ground could throw her entire balance off. Still, she kept on talking. "You're the one who wheeled himself out into the direct path of those... those creatures." She shuddered, pointing the direction the ugly, hairy hogs had gone. "That hog was coming straight for you."

"I was fine. I've been around hogs all my life. I know how to deal with them. But you coming outside while they were out here was not acceptable. You could have fallen and that hog would have gutted you."

She gasped, halting in front of him. "Gutted me. And you're telling me you would have been okay? I don't think so."

Wyatt's eyes flashed dangerously. "I would have been fine."

They glared at each other, seconds ticked by and slowly sanity seeped back to Amanda. What was she doing? She was behaving very unprofessionally. She'd just basically told him that he was an invalid and that was unforgivable. He had every right to be angry at her. "I'm sorry," she said quietly. "I'm way out of line. My only excuse is that I was really scared."

It was the truth. "I mean, I've never seen hogs that size. And when that one headed toward you all I could think of was *Old Yeller*—"

"I should have known," he groaned.

"Well, it was scary. The hogs killed that poor dog—"

"Amanda, you're here to help me get back on my feet. You are not here to get yourself hurt. Stay inside at night no matter what. Do you understand me?"

Loud and clear. "You are absolutely right. I'm going back to get a little more shut-eye right now." She held her fuzzy housecoat closer around her.

Wyatt's eyes glinted a hard warning. "Don't come outside again if you see hogs."

Just as mad as he was, she locked gazes with him. "I reacted without thinking to what I saw. Maybe it's you who needs to think about staying inside."

Wyatt's glare iced over. "I'm not kidding, Amanda."

And he thought she was? Hardly. "That makes two of us. Sleep well, Wyatt, because work begins at eight-thirty." Turning, she started carefully across the yard. The last thing she needed was for Wyatt to see her fall. From the standpoint of her pride, that wouldn't be good. And now wouldn't exactly be the opportune moment for him to realize she had only one leg. Maybe she should have told him earlier. But right now certainly wasn't a good time to reveal it…no telling how mad he'd be. Knowing Wyatt, he'd fire her all over again and this time she'd be gone for good.

Chapter Five

Wyatt sat on the back porch long after Amanda weaved her way back to the trailer. She was plucky, that was for certain—plucky enough to get herself into trouble. When she was safely back inside he breathed a sigh of relief. If that wild boar had headed her way, he'd have been hard-put to do anything to help her. He'd almost died of fright when she'd come outside yelling for him to get back.

What had he been thinking? He knew he'd put her in danger by his decision to come outside to run off the hogs. It would have been okay had he been standing and able to handle himself. With this hip injury he was useless. Of course he hadn't expected her to come outside, either. But that was beside the point—he shouldn't have come out here, plain and simple. He'd put them both in danger.

Disgusted, he spun the chair and drove back inside, letting the door slam behind him. He didn't even pretend that he was going to go back to sleep. He knew he wouldn't—he hadn't been sleeping ever since the crash. Instead he put on a pot of coffee and headed to the shower—and the ordeal that it represented to him. Standing for any length of time was hard. Getting dressed or undressed was trouble, too, often sending his back into spasms. Hopefully therapy would help.

Twenty minutes later, in pain, he poured himself a cup of coffee and headed to his desk, but he couldn't concentrate on the transcripts he was trying to go over.

Back before he'd crashed the plane, if he'd been disturbed about something when he was here, he'd have saddled a horse and gone for a ride across the pasture, even in the moonlight. Something about being in the saddle always helped ease his mind. He'd spent more time on horseback growing up than Cole and Seth put together. Then again, he'd helped out on the ranch from the day he'd turned eight. There was always something that could be done at almost any age and his dad had instilled a great work ethic in all of them. Those had been good days spent with his dad and his granddad, too. It was hard to realize how long it had been since both of them had passed away. First his granddad when a tractor had overturned on the side of a hill he was mowing. And then later his dad and mom when their plane had gone down over Missouri. He'd spent long hours in the saddle during those days. He'd been eighteen when his parents had died. When he'd become the head of the family. Being in the saddle had helped. In college he'd started running to do his thinking. He'd taken up flying then, too, much to his brothers' surprise. As odd as it seemed, being in the pilot's seat had helped him feel connected to his mom and dad. Now, all he could do was sit in this chair and stare out across the land.

The spasm grabbed him suddenly. As if he were being twisted apart by two different forces, the excruciating pain snarled through him, through his leg and upper body while the spasm tightened and jerked. Sweat popped across his forehead and despite trying not to, he groaned. Never in his life had he felt this weak. This out of control.

This scared.

There, he admitted it. The doctors had assured him he would recover, but he wanted out of this chair—the need to be out of it consumed him. The fear that it was all a lie worried him. He gripped the chair arms and fought off a wave of nausea as a flashback of waking up in the plane wreckage overcame him…the caustic smell of burning gas and oil hit him anew. He'd awakened to find himself trapped. He'd tried to move but couldn't, his legs were pinned. Blood had been everywhere and then the pain…even now he couldn't forget it. What he was feeling now was nothing. Needing to be free of the flashback, he forced memories away and drove his wheelchair to the kitchen. With an unsteady hand, he poured himself another cup of coffee, watching the pot shake as he did so.

Think of something good. His sister-in-law, Melody, had come over and made certain he could reach the things he needed.

That had been sweet of her. Seth had a great woman in his life. That was a very good thing.

He took a drink of the hot brew and felt the burn all the way to the pit of his stomach. *You are alive.*

The thought hovered about him in the silent kitchen.

It was a good thought. God had kept him alive in the wreckage of that tiny plane. Unlike his parents, his life had been spared. It was a miracle that he'd lived. He knew this. He should be grateful.

Instead he continued to feel at loose ends. Lost.

Wyatt had always known where he was going. What he wanted out of life and who he was as a man.

The truth was…something had changed in that wreckage. He'd lost something of himself and he wasn't sure how to get it back.

The alarm blasted at 7:30 a.m. Amanda woke from a dead sleep, cracked one eye open and glared at the clock. Normally she was a morning person, but not today. She groped for the alarm, shut it off and pushed herself up on her elbows then dropped onto her back. *Had she really had an encounter with wild hogs?*

Yup, it wasn't a nightmare. Wyatt had actually put himself in danger. The memory of that hog heading toward him flooded back to her, sending terror racing through her once more. Obstinate man!

No wonder she was so tired—being scared witless by ugly hogs and an irritating man would do that. And then to jump on her the way he had—the nerve of the man!

Yes, no doubt at all that they were going to grate on each other's nerves. She could see it coming as plain as day. Sighing, she sat up, threw her covers aside and rubbed the end of her leg. It was a habit she'd started right after she'd first lost her leg all those years ago. Her leg was gone but she still felt it. She'd gotten used to it now but still, the habit of rubbing the scar remained. Kind of like saying, "I haven't forgotten you." The kids liked the idea and had found comfort in knowing it was okay to miss the limb they'd lost. She yawned then stretched. Hopefully there would be no more hog incidents and she could get a good night's sleep tonight. She needed to not get too tired or she really would have a hard time dealing with Wyatt.

Wyatt. It was time to get up and get busy.

Thirty minutes later, after she'd showered and dressed, she felt wide-awake and ready to tackle her first day of work. She made her way across the shredded yard. It was amazing how bad it looked.

She found herself glancing toward the direction in which they'd vanished, making certain they didn't come charging out of the woods after her. She shivered. She'd lost her mind last night.

At the front door, she knocked. She'd begun to think he was asleep when he swung it open.

"Good morning," she said. He, too, looked as if he'd just showered. The hair at the back of his neck curled up slightly with dampness. Wyatt had great hair—not that it mattered to her, but he did have that run-your-fingers-through-his-hair sort of vibe going on.

Instead of returning her greeting, he gave her a quick nod and pointed to the phone earpiece he was wearing. "Yes," he said to the person on the other end as he whirled the wheelchair around and headed back down the hall, deep in conversation.

"Okey-dokey," she grunted under her breath. Entering the ancient building, she watched him disappear through the second doorway on the right. She peeked around the first doorway and saw that both openings led into the large living room/kitchen combo. Since he was on the phone, she decided to look at the wall of old photos in the hallway. There were many, many of them.

"I see you found the wall."

"Yes." She looked over her shoulder to where he'd reappeared in the doorway. She'd been so intent on the pictures that she hadn't realized his conversation had ended. "These are wonderful. I feel like I'm in a museum." Would he hold the hog incident against her?

"It is in a way. Those are all authentic. We don't know who many of them are, but Melody is trying to figure that out. Being a history teacher, she's really interested in discovering who everyone is."

"That's awesome. I'm afraid my family knows nothing of its history past my great-grandfather." Obviously they were going to ignore the hog incident and move forward.

He looked tired and she wondered if he'd slept much. It dawned on her that he might have been up before the hog attack.

His gaze ran down the length of the photos. "If it hadn't been for the fact that I was born into a family whose history had been so documented because of this place then I probably wouldn't know anything, either. I'm proud of it, though. This ranch represents a lot of hard work and dedication."

He was halfway through this conversation when it dawned on her that they were actually carrying on a decent conversation. She wanted it to keep on; maybe talking about family was a way to pull him out. "So what exactly do you know about your family?"

He shifted in the chair. "This ranch has our roots in it six generations back."

"Really?"

His lip hitched on one side. "My great-great-great-great-great-grandpa Oakley won this stagecoach house in a poker game."

She laughed. "Get-out-a-here! A poker game."

"That's right. Ole Oakley was a card. He

didn't have the best reputation around and was a horse trader, too. Word is you never knew if you were getting a stolen horse or not. But he could spin a tall tale and convince anyone to do what he wanted. He was also a man with a perfect poker face. Thus the winning of this place. Can you imagine throwing away your livelihood in one roll of the dice?"

"No, I can't," she said.

"Pretty sorry, if you ask me."

"I agree. So he won this and then what?" She was totally interested in this conversation but she was also thankful for the opportunity to visit with Wyatt.

"He moved his wife and son here and they ran the stop for years. There were only seventy acres with the stagecoach house, but Oakley's son, Mason, married a girl whose family owned the rest. Through the years each generation has added land as it came available."

Wyatt's phone rang and he answered it. Obviously it was his office again. She wondered how much work he was still doing. She lingered in the hall a few more minutes and then gave up hope that he would hang up anytime soon. She walked into the living room/kitchen. Their gazes met as he pointed to the coffeepot. She shook her head, which he barely acknowledged as his full attention was drawn to the phone conversation. Finally, after a lot of talk that sounded like something out of an episode of *Law and Order,* he hung up. But from what she'd gathered he was about to receive a ton of casework to review.

"So it sounds like you're working hard." She tried to hold back the censure in her voice but it was impossible. He was, after all, the high achiever who probably thought the office wouldn't continue to function without him.

"Consulting on a case with a junior partner."

"I hope that doesn't get in the way of our therapy."

"Nothing will get in the way of that," he assured her, his jaw tightening as he spoke. "Nothing is more important than me getting out of this chair and back on my feet."

They stared at each other across the old wooden kitchen table as a heavy silence cloaked the space between them. "Good." She was used to having confrontations with her clients over cell phone usage during workouts—texting their friends or surfing the Web. She was used to them being fresh-faced teens or younger, not a handsome man with challenge in his gaze. Telling him how to behave felt totally uncomfortable, since there was no obvious doubt that he didn't appreciate her interference. "I guess we should get started," she said, attempting to diffuse the tension between them. This was her job and she needed to do it. "Where is the room we'll be using for the therapy?"

"Across the hall." He led the way into what had probably been a bedroom but now held an assortment of workout equipment.

"You have a regular fitness center in here."

He stopped his chair in the center of the room. "I wasn't sure what we would need, so I had everything brought in."

Was that embarrassment she was seeing?

There was a bench press, a state of the art universal machine, a treadmill that looked like it could do everything for you—even walk for you. There was a massage table center stage and a rolling cart with towels and room for anything she'd brought. "The table is great." She moved over to it. "This is where we need to start this morning. I'm going to evaluate your situation and then we'll get started with your treatment. How does that therapeutic massage sound this morning?"

His forehead crinkled—cutely. "Now *that* I can get excited about."

"If you'll get up here, we'll get started." A beeping sound came from another room in the house and then the distinct sound of a fax working as pages came through.

"Let me check that."

He was gone before she could say anything. She had the distinct feeling she was going to have to compete with his office. She wasn't going to jump to conclusions just yet because he'd sounded so determined yesterday.

She had the massage table prepped when he came back ten minutes later.

"Do I need to help you?" She got a quick shake of the head in answer and watched as he stood. Putting all his weight on the one leg, he balanced on his good leg. His face told more than he probably wanted it to about the pain he was experiencing.

She knew it was hard for a man like him to ask for help, so she held back but still took a step forward. There was nothing weak looking about him. He had on gym shorts and his well-developed calves had a good dusting of dark hair and were tanned enough for her to pretty much know he jogged outside—if he was a jogger like she suspected he was.

She started to ask him, but he turned too quickly, winched in pain and lost his balance. If he'd had the use of his left arm, he would have reached out for the table to help him regain his balance, but he didn't. One minute he was standing, the next he was toppling. Once again, Amanda reacted on instinct. Heart pumping, she scooted into the line of what seemed like a toppling oak tree and wrapped her arm around his waist. "Here we go," she gasped, looking up at him. Relieved she'd gotten to him.

His good arm curled about her shoulders for support. "Don't hurt yourself," he grunted.

"I won't." Amanda concentrated on her own balance and not on the fact that Wyatt's arm was around her and hers around him. He smelled great—

"Nothing like being a klutz," he ground out.

Amanda laughed. Poor man was so out of

his comfort zone needing help. Especially help from a woman. She squeezed his waist encouragingly. "I feel your pain," she told him as she met his eyes. Their faces were so close. Her nerves jangled like alarms, and looking at him, she felt breathless. Goodness. She couldn't look away as his gaze dropped from her eyes to her lips then shot back up to hold hers. Her breath caught. She was close enough to see the iridescent blue flecks encircling his darker blue irises.

They both reacted at the same time. He dropped his arm, but she was already moving away. Putting the table between them, she gave a weak smile. "You're not a klutz." A hunk, no doubt about it, but not a klutz. "You're doing great."

He scowled. "I've managed until now to not fall on my face. And I don't need to break your back or your leg in the process of doing it now." And just like that he slammed a door between them as he sat down on the edge of the massage table.

"You didn't," she snapped. Flustered from the encounter and not exactly sure how to deal with it, Amanda set to work evaluating his shoulder. What was she doing—she'd just been dumped by her fiancé, and yet here she was noticing how amazingly attractive her new client was. It was disturbing on so many levels and very much unlike her.

"So what's the verdict?" Wyatt asked finally when it looked like he wasn't going to speak. Amanda had clammed up after he'd almost crushed her—and what was with him? He'd found himself almost drowning in her eyes when he'd looked down at her. He'd forgotten himself for a minute. But he wouldn't have lost his balance if his hip hadn't seized up on him. That was all it took to remind him Amanda was going to help him walk again. And that was the only thing he needed to be thinking about where she was concerned.

Only problem he found with that line of thinking: doing it. Not easy with her poking and prodding his shoulder with gentle, efficient fingers. *Twelve years.*

Their age difference wouldn't have seemed so vast a difference before the plane crash. But right now, it was generations. He'd never been one to date women more than a couple of years younger than him.

He'd always found women his own age to be more in touch with life as he enjoyed it.

"Lift your arm, please," she asked, breaking the silence. Holding her hand out, she waited for him to do as she asked.

He raised his arm but couldn't get it as high as her hand, which was about midway between his elbow and shoulder.

"Fine. On a scale of one to ten, what's the pain?"

"About a seven," he managed.

"On the conservative side?" she asked with a knowing look. One that said she knew exactly how bad he hurt.

He nodded, letting her know she was right as he let his arm down. His shoulder throbbed.

After a few more questions and then some evaluation of his hip and back she finally moved away, giving him some much-needed space. The woman was all business and he liked the way she worked. Her serious expression belied her attractiveness as she asked questions and jotted notes. Impressive.

"Just as I'd thought from reviewing your charts," she said. "We'll start with some simple, isolation exercises to help the rotator cuff. It will show steady improvement as we go and you really shouldn't need that sling for long. The doctors put you in it just so you wouldn't strain it any more before we could get started working. That might help you sleep better."

He rubbed his jaw. His shoulder wasn't what was keeping him awake at night or pushing him to find ways to keep his mind occupied. Bad dreams were doing a bang-up job of that all on their own. "That'd be good," he said, and though he knew it wasn't going to help him sleep, he was ready to ditch the sling and not put it back on. "You can burn it right now and I won't complain."

She smiled and her doe eyes twinkled. "I'll give you that honor if you'd like. You just have to promise me you won't overuse your arm or I'll have to make you wear the sling again."

"Scout's honor I'll behave."

"Good. With the hip and back it'll take more time, but the good news is you'll be up and out of that chair in less than two weeks. Then the real work will begin. You have nothing to be worried about, though, you will mend."

He let her words sink in. The doctors had said the same thing, but he hadn't believed them. Not with the pain he was experiencing. "You're sure?" He felt vulnerable voicing the question but the fact that Amanda had been through what she'd been through made him pretty sure she understood his hesitancy in believing.

Amanda crossed her arms, leaned her head to the side and gave him an assuring look. "I'm sure. You just have to give it your all. That hip is going to complain, but I'll help with those spasms and every day it will get better."

Only time would tell whether his putting his trust in Amanda was well-founded—but he did feel encouraged. And that was a good feeling. "Then let's get busy. Results are what I'm interested in. I'd like to make that two into one."

"Realistically, I don't see that happening." She gave him a frank look, her lips curved upward gently. "But for some reason I get the feeling that when you set your mind to something you make it happen."

Thoughts of the crash flashed across his mind. He rubbed his temple but it didn't ease the throbbing behind his eyes. "Yeah, that's me. I get it done."

Chapter Six

"So how are y'all getting along?" Seth asked Wyatt on the second day after Amanda's arrival. He'd insisted on bringing the tractor over to smooth out the ground destroyed by the hogs.

Fighting a spasm shooting through him from his hip, Wyatt hid a grimace from Seth. "We get along fine."

Seth didn't look impressed by his answer. "Fine? I don't like the sound of that. Are you still giving her a hard time?"

"We'll be fine, Seth. Stop worrying. If she doesn't get herself killed acting impulsively like she did last night."

"What did she do?"

"She came out of her trailer when all the hogs were in the yard."

Seth looked alarmed. "Why would she do a fool thing like that? She could have fallen—" He clamped his mouth shut midsentence and frowned. "Did she tell you about her accident?"

"You mean being hit by a drunk driver?" Wyatt asked, wondering what was wrong with Seth.

"Yeah," Seth said. "What did she say?"

"That she was hurt badly—almost killed—and had to be homeschooled."

"Did she say what her injuries were?"

"No. I didn't ask her to elaborate. I'm sure if she'd wanted to talk about it she would have told me. That must have been horribly traumatic for a kid her age." He knew what he was going through with his nightmares. "Why, did you read about it in her file?"

Seth looked angry. "Yeah. She didn't have any business out there with those hogs."

Wyatt felt remorse. "I can't let her take all the blame. I was on the porch and one of them headed my way. She thought I was about to be run over by the thing and I guess she thought she could save me."

"What were you thinking? You're in a wheelchair, Wyatt. And she could have really been hurt. That's a little different than when you, me and Cole used to hunt those things. What were you planning to do? Play chicken with them? Wrestle them with one arm?"

Maybe he shouldn't have admitted his guilt and avoided this dose of reality. He hadn't had a clue what he was going to do once he got out there… "I'd have handled it," he snapped. "The important thing was that Amanda came charging out there in the middle of them and could have been injured—she could have gotten knocked down. At least they were too busy trying to get away to hurt her. Still, the crazy one that was coming at me could have turned on her."

"So I guess you jumped her pretty bad?"

"Not too bad. But she doesn't take criticism too well."

"Ha!" Seth laughed. "You and her have something in common."

Wyatt shot him a scowl.

"It's true and you know it."

"She's not happy that I'm working, either."

"She *tell* you that?"

"She might as well have. It was written all over her face the moment she found out."

A wide grin spread across Seth's face

along with a teasing glint that could only be described as a Turner trait through and through. "Why does this woman bug you so much? You are irritated about everything having to do with her."

Wyatt prickled. "Hey, you and Cole were the ones that hired her. I still don't know what you two knuckleheads were thinking. She's too young. And for the most part, she's only worked with kids. She is totally not right for this job. The hog incident proved that. And yet she's here. Why is that?"

"Because, big bro, we had hired someone else who had to back out for family reasons. Amanda was—well, bluntly, she was a last resort. But her boss assured us that she was far more capable than the other physical therapist to handle your case. So we took her. You're just going to have to straighten up and fly right. It's going to be great."

Yeah, right. He'd believe that when he saw it. "And she doesn't bug me. It's not personal. She just isn't right for the job." Well it was a little personal. But he sure wasn't opening his big mouth again and saying that.

Seth gave him a look of complete disbelief. "You are so bothered by this woman that it isn't even funny. All those other excuses aside, I'm curious if it has anything to do with the fact that you find her attractive. She's pretty, got grit and enough determination that I figured you'd like her."

"She's *twelve* years younger than me—"

"So. You're not in high school anymore. It doesn't matter."

Wyatt disagreed. Yeah, sure, no doubt about it—he did find his physical therapist attractive. "Twelve years is too big a difference to me. I'm not looking to date Amanda anyway. She's here for a job and all I want right now is to get mobile. That's more important than a date."

For some reason, Seth's grin told him he wasn't buying any of that. Too bad. "Stop grinning, brother, and get back on that tractor and smooth out this ground."

"She seems to get along really well...I mean, you know, since being in such bad shape."

"She does. That drunk driver almost killed her and had no injuries. It's criminal."

Wyatt had been careless in flying his plane when he shouldn't have. "I'm grateful that my plane crash didn't harm anyone other than me," he said remorsefully. "I wouldn't have been able to live with that. What if I'd killed someone?" The idea made him ill. His gut clenched and his back started tightening up. He knew any minute it would seize up and put him in a world of pain.

"I hadn't thought of that," Seth said, all humor evaporated. "Wyatt, it's not the same thing. You didn't knowingly have that crash and you weren't drinking and flying. I hope you don't hold that against yourself. It was an accident. That's all. Just like Mom and Dad's crash."

Wyatt grimaced against the pain shooting through him and fought to hide it. "I knew better than to go up in the middle of a storm like that. That makes me liable in my book. It was a straightforward act of negligence. It's different than Dad. His crash was on a clear day. He did nothing stupid."

Seth looked away, studying the ground as he thought of a comeback. Wyatt knew that deep down Seth had to agree. Seth was too responsible, too black and white where right and wrong were concerned not to see it Wyatt's way. It was only his protective instincts for Wyatt that had him making excuses.

"You can agree with me," Wyatt said. "You know good and well that you tried to talk me out of it. I should have listened."

Seth took a deep breath, thumbed his Stetson back off his forehead and looked at him with worried eyes. "Come on, Wyatt, maybe that's all well and true. But you have to snap out of this mode of thinking. It's eating you up. You can't keep second-guessing your decision. You took off in the middle of that storm—you'd done it before with no problems. You're one of the best twin-engine pilots around. You've never had an incident before—and that time when you had engine malfunctions you got that plane back to the airstrip on a wing and a prayer, basically. This happened because it happened. Period. Let it go and get on with it."

Wyatt closed his eyes against the pain ripping through him and the images of being trapped started playing across his mind. Not good. He opened his eyes to meet Seth's studying him with concern. "I'm fine, Seth. Stop worrying."

"You aren't and we both know it. I'm

going to smooth out this ground, then head back home. My advice to you is to lighten up. Stop thinking about how you lost control—you and I both have a problem with control. God is in control even when we think we're the ones doing the driving. God has a plan. You can't see what that is right now, but believe me, He can. I learned that the hard way. Just go with the flow and get yourself well. Stop looking back and blaming yourself and thank God that you didn't hurt anyone else in that crash. And by all means do what your pretty physical therapist is telling you to do so you'll get back to being yourself."

Wyatt wasn't sure if he'd ever get back to being himself. What Seth said was true. He'd found out in that crash just how easily and quickly control could be lost.

Seth started to walk away toward the tractor but stopped. "There was only one perfect man and his name was Jesus. You're human, Wyatt. Always have been, always will be. Humans all make mistakes, so give yourself a break, won't ya? Cole won't get married until you're able to stand up and be his best man. He's counting on you to be there for him body and spirit."

Wyatt watched Seth head across the yard toward the tractor. Catching Seth's grin as he climbed up into the seat, Wyatt was reminded of how strong Seth had been during the deaths of their parents. The serious one, Seth had always been steady and true. Sometimes too serious, but always the one with wisdom beyond his years. Wyatt knew Seth's advice was as true now as it always was, but right now, with the things going on in his head, taking that advice wasn't as cut-and-dried as it should be.

"Hey, big brother, while you're working on standing up, forget about those twelve years and get to know Amanda. She seems like the kind of gal who might be great for you."

"Mow, Seth." That advice he wouldn't take. Right now the last thing he needed to be thinking about was a woman.

Seth plopped into the seat. "Hey, I'm goin', but I'm just sayin'—"

"And I'm just sayin' *mow*." Wyatt thought about Amanda and knew that if she heard what Seth was saying she'd probably laugh her way off the property and back to San Antonio...and well-warranted on her part.

* * *

"So, why don't you work with kids anymore? Did you get tired of it?"

The question took Amanda by surprise. She was standing in the kitchen taking a chicken casserole out of the oven. Earlier that day, Seth's wife, Melody, and Cole's fiancée, Susan, had stopped by to meet her. They'd come bearing food and warm welcomes. Melody was a history teacher and Susan was a veterinarian. They hadn't stayed long but she'd enjoyed meeting them. Wyatt visited with them some, but after they left he'd immediately gone back to being about as communicative as a rock for the rest of therapy. And now he wanted to ask her *this?* Of all things to want to talk about.

She set the hot dish on the burner to cool and then removed her oven mitts as she debated exactly how to answer his question. "No. I didn't get tired of it. I just needed a change."

She reached inside the cabinet and pulled out a plate for him and one for herself—to take back to her trailer like she'd been doing since she arrived. She could feel his blue eyes on her and had to make herself not feel self-conscious. The fact that she found him attractive bothered her. It didn't help matters at all. Call her daft and it would fit.

"I thought you told me the other day that you loved your work."

The man remembered way too much of their conversation in detail. "I did." She weighed her options. She wasn't going to tell him about not being able to have children, but she needed to tell him something. "Look, I was supposed to get married and my fiancé decided he didn't want to. That tends to make you need a change of scenery. I decided coming here to Mule Hollow for a few months was a good idea." There, that was about the best answer she could stand to give. It was the truth, too. Just not all the details.

She dished the chicken and rice onto his plate, glancing at him when he didn't say anything. He had an intense expression on his face as he watched her.

"That had to be rough." His voice gentled.

His compassion was unexpected. "Yes," she said, inhaling slowly, trying to steady her rattled nerves. "It was. But it is what it is. I'm better off knowing up front."

"True, but that doesn't make it hurt less."

She stared at him briefly, startled all the more. With shaking hands, she dished her own meal onto the plate then grabbed the foil, ripped a piece off and covered her food with it. She needed to go home—to her trailer across the yard. "But I have my work and that's a good thing," she finally said, hoping he didn't ask too many more questions. Hoping he let it go at that. She wasn't ready for questions.

Not from him, anyway.

Wyatt studied Amanda and wondered what she was hiding. He'd been thinking about their conversation a lot, though he'd tried not to.

"So you're here to work. To escape?" What was he doing?

She set his plate on the table beside the glass of tea and the neatly folded napkin. She'd taken care with the place setting and now she straightened the napkin—despite that it didn't need it. She was upset, nervous. He waited to see what else she said. Nervous people talked if you kept quiet and gave them room.

"I guess I could deny it but there isn't really any reason to. Yes. I'm here to work and forget and…" She took a step back and smiled, though it didn't reach her eyes. No, her eyes were too bright. "Well, anyway, here's your supper. I'm going to head over to my house." She turned away and grabbed her plate. She was almost in tears.

Wyatt had the impulse to ask her to stay and talk more—but it was clear talking about it upset her, so he didn't. She wasn't ready. And this was more personal than he wanted to get….

But how had a man hurt her like that?

He forced himself to move his chair up to the table. "Thanks for the supper," he said, clamping down on his natural instinct to dig deeper. Now wasn't the time…and it wasn't his business anyway.

She barely looked at him. "You're welcome. Call if you need anything."

He watched her go. Her shiny dark hair swung in time to her step as she moved. Why had her fiancé dumped her? It didn't matter really, because she was better off without him if he didn't love her. It was evident that she'd loved him, though—still did, from the way she'd reacted. Her emotion had been real. Her heartache was evident; Wyatt didn't like seeing her pain. But she was right—her work would help her escape. To cope, at least, just as his was helping him.

Chapter Seven

Amanda hurried out of Wyatt's as though the house was on fire. She shouldn't have talked about Jonathan. She hadn't planned on telling anyone—especially Wyatt. And now she'd gone and opened up to him like that, when keeping her mouth shut would have been the better way.

Anxious, she sank into the kitchen chair of her travel trailer and felt the walls closing in on her. She'd laid her Bible beside her bed when she'd unpacked, but she hadn't opened it. Now she reached for it, feeling an urgent need.

But, like all the other times she'd tried to read since the breakup, she couldn't do it. It felt like there was a barrier between her and the words written on the page. Oh, she could scan them, but it was as if someone was speaking and she was inside a soundproof room, hearing nothing. She closed the book and, needing space, she went outside.

She walked to the rear of the trailer, not wanting Wyatt to see her pacing. She'd seen what looked like a low wall near the wood's edge and she was pleasantly surprised to find an archway with an iron gate. The hinges squeaked as she pulled the gate open, and with a feeling of excitement she found stone steps leading down the hill.

How old were the wall and steps?

She could hear rushing water and she carefully followed the steps downward toward the sound. Through the trees she saw the river—it was as restless looking as she felt as it swept by in a swirling mass. At the base of the steps she found a large rock that jutted out over the water. She went to the rock and stared down at the turbulent water.

Though the water swirled and rolled, it was a peaceful place. And it was absolutely beautiful. Huge oak trees lined the banks behind her. In front of her, the rock she stood on connected to a long formation that caused the river to narrow. It was a great place. She moved down the wide rock and found a place to sit. Surely she could think here.

She'd allowed herself to cross that line, thinking about Jonathan. He'd realized there was so much more out there that he could have without her. How could she blame him when even she knew he was right? Sucking in a shaky breath, she felt a tear roll down her cheek and brushed it aside. *Dear Lord, help me get through this.* The prayer came to her, a plea more than a prayer. And all she could do was hope God would answer her.

Wyatt was on the phone when Amanda poked her head through the door the next morning. She still couldn't believe she'd told him about Jonathan. She knew Wyatt probably hadn't missed how upset she'd been. Or that she hadn't turned her light off much that night…he hadn't turned his off until early morning.

She needed work today—not conversation. One look at his face told her he was in extreme pain.

"Looks like you really need me today." She felt for him as she headed toward the therapy room. "Let's get you on the table and after we ease up some of that agony you're in, we'll work on the ligature of that hip. Then, if you're up to it, we'll get started on your arm."

"Give me a minute," he said, distracted. "I need to make another call." He was already dialing the number when she turned back to glare at him from the doorway.

He looked worn out on top of being in pain, and she was in no mood to let things slide. "You're hurting and you need to relax. Period."

His expression darkened. "I said I'll hang up in a minute. This is important."

Amanda slammed her fists to her hips. "Right now your well-being is the most important thing in your life. And the *only* thing I'm interested in. This work you're doing isn't my priority. How many cases are you working on, anyway? You can't tell me all these phone calls and all that paperwork is just one case."

He didn't answer, just stared at her like she'd lost it. Maybe she had, because she just kept right on going. "Are you consulting on the cases of the entire law firm? Don't these people know you need time off to heal?"

He looked perplexed. "I'm working because I want to. And because these are my cases that have had to be borne on someone else's shoulders. I need to see them through."

"Well, I need to see your therapy through. So hang that phone up right now."

He was in shock. His expression was one she'd seen on her teenage patients when she'd threatened to take away their phones. It was a combination of disbelief and irritation. "I'm not joking, Wyatt. As your physical therapist I'm telling you that you need to put your health first and get in here on this table."

Not looking happy at all, he set the phone down and drove his wheelchair past her into the PT room.

Amanda prayed for patience as she followed him. She never expected this to be easy, and in reality she'd had far worse rebellion from some kids who took their pain and loss out on her. She'd eventually helped them and she would do the same with Wyatt. Yesterday she'd let him see her get emotional, personal. That had been a mistake.

She waited as he removed his shirt and got settled on the table. His muscles rippled as he did so, drawing her attention. The man was something—even with the fresh scars on his back. He didn't say a word and she was fine with that. She needed to keep this strictly business. Her mind couldn't dwell on his muscles in any way, shape or form other than the ones she was here to fix.

She got to work, focused on it and, like she had the other times when she'd given him his massage, she refrained from asking him anything about his accident. She figured if he wanted to talk about it he would. The red scars ran down his back on his left side, and there were also some on his arm and chest.

From the heating unit she took heated pads and applied them to his back and hip then covered them with warm towels.

"Just relax and let the heat loosen you up," she said, then went to the small desk and opened his chart. One thing she was glad about was that he hadn't pursued his line of questioning today.

She'd had a rough night after telling him about Jonathan. Sleep hadn't helped— what little she'd had was restless. She'd awakened more tired, it seemed, than when she'd closed her eyes.

Her gaze wandered back to where Wyatt lay covered in towels with his head down staring at the floor through the hole in the table.

"Your place is beautiful," she said, suddenly needing conversation. "I found the stone stairway yesterday evening."

"You went down by the river?"

"Yes. It was almost like being swept back in time sitting down there. I wonder how old that stairway is?"

"At least a hundred and fifty years—like the house. I think it was all done at the same time."

"Amazing." When he said nothing she filled in. "Those who passed this way over the years must have felt a sense of peace when they arrived here." She'd felt it briefly. Very briefly.

"That's what I always thought."

She didn't have anything to fill the silence with this time.

Wyatt shifted on the table. "I've always loved it here."

That she'd gathered from others' conversations. "Why did you move away?" The personal question was out before she realized it. But she was curious and she did need something to take her mind off her own troubles. Seconds clicked by as if he, too, was unsure about wanting to continue conversing.

"I've always wanted to be a lawyer," he offered finally.

"Oh." She searched for something to ask. Why had she initiated the conversation?

"Are you always so bossy?"

She was grateful for the unexpected question even if it was grunted. "My momma says yes."

He raised his head from the table and looked at her. "I have a feeling she's right."

She could see it in his eyes that he was still in pain and she wasn't sure whether he was talking to distract himself from it. But he didn't need to be looking at her. "Put that head back down. You still have five minutes."

He ignored her. "So what was this sorry guy's problem?"

This was not the conversation she wanted to have. "He wasn't sorry."

"What?" Wyatt pushed up from the table with his good arm. "If that's the case, then what did you do?"

She crossed to him and started hastily removing the heating pads. "Nothing. Can we not talk about this?" Why had she said that? It would only spike his curiosity further.

She pushed him down and started working on his back. "So are wild hogs the norm around here? Am I going to have to dodge them?" She hadn't begun her early morning jogs, but knew it was time. She needed the release jogging gave her. But the wild hog incident had put a damper on that and...in actuality she just hadn't been able to make herself get out of bed like she usually did. She knew getting back into it would help her feel better.... She just wasn't sure about jogging alone in the pastures at the crack of dawn.

"Seth has trappers come periodically to keep them down. Most every rancher has problems with them. So you might run into them, but not likely in the daytime. Why, are you planning on starting to trap them?"

"*Hardly.* I really don't want to have anything to do with those mean-looking things."

"Good. They might be back during the night at some point and if so, no matter what, you need to stay inside. But you probably won't see any during daylight hours."

"You're sure?" She didn't want to specifically mention that she was going to be running early in the morning and that they scared her a little. Okay, a lot. She was a coward. She *was* running tomorrow. Pigs or no pigs, she was going to pull herself out of this state of lethargy. She knew it was all the oppressed emotions dragging her down. She'd hoped work would help, but so far nothing had helped. Not even God.

"You're loosening up. Is the pain ebbing?" She was glad to feel him relax with each motion of her hands.

"It's a dull ache right now."

"You'll be glad to know that we're stepping it up today. We're going to push harder and then we'll get cracking on standing up. You're in great shape, so that's going to work to your advantage." No doubt about it, Wyatt was in *excellent* shape.

"Hey!" he yelped when she hit a sore spot.

"Sorry!" *Focus, Amanda! Focus!* "I thought I had that worked out of there."

"That's okay." He grunted and shifted uncomfortably. "Just wasn't expecting it."

"So are you a runner?" She asked the first thing that came to mind, venturing another personal question. When he was talking he seemed to loosen up quicker.

"Before the plane crash, I jogged every day. Plus, I worked out at the gym. It helped with my mental acuity. It's good to know all that work wasn't for nothing."

So he was a jogger just like she'd thought. "Getting in shape is never for nothing. Have you run any marathons?"

"I did the Alcatraz Iron Man Triathlon last year. That was my first venture into competitive running."

"Your first venture!" Amanda said in disbelief. "You tackled a swim from Alcatraz, topped it off with biking and running for your *first* venture. I am in awe."

"Don't be," he drawled, glancing over his shoulder at her. "I came in middle of the pack in my age group."

The way he said that said it all. He'd gone out to come in first on his very first marathon race. The man had high expectations for himself. To him, middle of the pack was as bad as coming in last. It was all or nothing for Wyatt Turner.

"I'm still impressed."

He grunted. "I'm not."

She worked in silence for the next few minutes. He seemed content to relax and let her work.

Finally she asked him to flip to his back and she placed her fingers beneath his ankle again. "Lift, please. Good. Now, this time I'm going to rotate it. How does that feel?"

"Tight."

"In other words, it still hurts."

"That is correct," he said, tense.

She smiled at the lawyerly way he'd answered. Not a yes, but: *that is correct.* "It is getting better. But during the next few weeks pushing your limits will mean pain," she warned. "It's the only way to gain full range of motion."

He didn't hesitate at that, but gave her a boyish grin. "If it takes you beating me up every day in order for me to gain back my 'full range of motion,' then have at it, Doc. You have my full cooperation."

Startled by his smile, Amanda felt lighter suddenly. But *full cooperation.* She'd believe that when she saw it.

Chapter Eight

Amanda decided to drive into town during her break that afternoon and check out some of the shops. It was a beautiful Saturday and she felt a little lighter after her morning session with Wyatt. They'd made progress in more ways than one this morning. Her heart had been lifted during their conversation. She knew she made him feel some relief, also, by the time she'd left. Not just physically but mentally. That may have come strictly from the fact that he was about to start putting some weight on his hip. Forward motion for him was all he cared about. She knew the lightness in her heart that had hit her when he'd smiled at her had come from the fact that she loved to see her patients feeling better.

The memory of that boyish grin replayed across her mind all afternoon, though. Each time it did she found herself smiling. Just like she was doing now.

She parked in front of Heavenly Inspirations hair salon. The bright pink building could be seen all the way from the crossroads, a beacon for the town. The pink car sitting in front of it did the same. It was one of those Elvis Cadillacs, the kind from the 1950s with the shark-tail fenders. Who did it belong to? No telling, since there seemed to be a good amount of folks in town today.

Cars lined the street and a chattering group was heading into the diner that very minute. And at Pete's, the feed store directly across from the salon, there were three trucks backed up. Cowboys were loading big sacks of feed into the beds. As she was standing there, she noticed a sign on the window of the salon. There was going to be a roping event at the Matlock Ranch Arena the following Saturday. Amanda was thinking that this sounded like fun when the salon door was flung open and a small woman with a head of very blond hair stepped outside.

"Hey there! I'm Lacy Matlock." She held

out her hand and smiled. Her hair was about three inches long all over her head and looked like she'd just stepped out of a wind tunnel. It was tousled this way and that way and looked really cute on the perky gal whose blue, blue eyes were twinkling with warmth. "You're Amanda, the one working out at Wyatt's, aren't you?"

"Yes." Amanda shook Lacy's hand. "How did you know?"

"Norma Sue and Esther Mae described you to me perfectly and when I saw you through the window, I knew it had to be you."

Amanda couldn't help smiling at the bubbly blonde. She was the kind of person who made you feel good just by being near them. She was animated with joy and energy, smiling and waving her orange-tipped fingernails about as she talked. "Should I ask how they described me or should I be afraid?"

"Oh, it's all good. Believe me, those two liked you the minute they saw you. Which only got better when they found out you were here to take care of their boy."

"Their boy?"

"They claim Wyatt, Cole and Seth. They

claim all the cowboys within the seventy-mile radius around Mule Hollow, but those Turner men practically grew up at their houses. They were real close with Wyatt's parents."

"Oh, I see. That explains why they were so excited that I was here to take care of Wyatt."

"Yep. They have been so worried about Wyatt. And they have been talking nonstop since you arrived. How are you doing? Are y'all getting along all right?"

How did she answer that? "We're getting used to each other." That was the truth.

Lacy's expression grew compassionate. "He's been through a lot, I'm guessing he's still having a hard time dealing with the situation. Even with the blessing of being alive, men don't enjoy being tied down. My Clint would be like a penned-up bull if he couldn't get out and tend to his ranch." She patted her small rounded stomach. "And I'm sure our baby will be the same way."

"I'm sure you are really excited about the baby even if he or she is a ball of energy."

"Oh, yeah, that is for certain. We have wanted a baby for a long time. God finally said the timing was right and here we are, waiting for the happy day. I'm loving every minute of it."

Amanda decided to open up a bit but didn't feel right saying too much. "Wyatt is having a hard time. But each day he's getting further along."

Lacy checked her watch. "Are y'all going to try and get out some? He's not even been to church since he was injured. We'd love to have y'all come tomorrow. Or even if Wyatt doesn't want to get out, we'd love to see you."

"You know, I hadn't thought about going to church just yet, but that is actually a wonderful idea. It would get Wyatt out of the house and get him around people who care for him." She hadn't thought of it because she was still trying to deal with her own faith issues.

"And God will be pleased to see y'all there as much as we will be."

"I think that's a great idea, Lacy." It would be good for him…and for her.

"Well, I need to run, I've got a color client under the dryer and her time is almost up…" She hesitated before turning back to the door. "Amanda, I normally wouldn't say this, but you're right, coming to church will be good for him. I think Wyatt is angry with himself and I just think he needs some peace. Connecting with God and fellowshipping with his church family will help him."

That struck Amanda hard—almost as if Lacy had hit her with a rock, because that was exactly what was wrong with Wyatt— not to mention that *she* needed peace, too…but this was about Wyatt. She'd known something had him hiding in his work. *And* something had him moody—he just didn't strike her as the kind of man who would normally be moody. He'd almost died and he was stuck in a wheelchair. That was enough to make anyone moody. But she was curious as to what Lacy's thoughts were. "Why do you think that?"

Lacy shrugged. "It's just, I was with my husband, who is a first responder on our volunteer fire department, so I was there when they pulled him out. He was barely conscious. I mean, it was a miracle that he wasn't harmed worse. A miracle and good flying skills. He landed that plane in the middle of a horrible storm in a very bad area. It wasn't as if he were in open pasture but rather a tree-covered spot near some of the hills we have in Texas Hill Country. God had to have had His hand on that plane. I think maybe that is what could be worrying Wyatt. He kept mumbling that he'd been stupid and arrogant—I don't even know if he remembers that he said that. When we all got to him, he was in such bad shape. He'd lost a good bit of blood." Lacy stopped speaking suddenly and looked uncomfortable. "I'm sorry. I know it's hard to believe since I'm the town hairstylist and salons are the gossip mills of small towns, but I really don't do this normally. It's just I get the sense that maybe you need to know this. Come tomorrow if you can. Everyone would love to meet you. And just give me a call if you need anything."

Amanda watched as Lacy practically flew back into her salon. She'd spent less than fifteen minutes talking and she felt as if she'd known Lacy all her life. There was something about her that made a person know she genuinely cared.

Amanda liked that. She liked feeling like she was among folks who looked out for each other. She stared down the sidewalk at the tiny town and, as she had that first day, she wondered what it would be like to just move here. Would that be considered running away from her problems?

"Tomorrow is Sunday and I thought we'd go to church," Amanda said when they'd started their afternoon session. Once again, Wyatt had been buried in research when she'd arrived.

Now he shot her a scowl. "I'm not going to church. No way."

So much for full cooperation—of course she'd seen that already. *"Yes way."*

He'd been okay during the therapy after she'd been firm, but he hadn't been very talkative that afternoon. Again she wasn't happy about his workload but had decided to hold her tongue. For now, anyway. She processed the information Lacy had given her. "When was the last time you got out of this house?"

"I haven't left since they brought me home and I'm not going to church in that *chair*."

So that was it. "It will do you good."

"Forget it, Amanda."

"Look." She could be just as stubborn as he could be. "This is part of therapy. Getting out and about will be good for you. You have gotten too tied to these four walls surrounding you. And way too connected to your phone."

He glared at her, his dark brows crinkled and almost touching in the middle. "I'm not going out in that stinkin' chair. Get it out of your head."

His words hit Amanda wrong. She fought down her temper. Did he not know how blessed he was? Did he think he was too good to be seen in a wheelchair? Irritated beyond words, she glared right back at him. "I don't know if you've noticed," she gritted through clenched teeth. "No, you probably haven't since you've been too busy feeling sorry for yourself. But there is an abundance of people who live *every* single day of their lives in wheelchairs. For them there is no hope of ever getting out of 'that chair,' as you so callously call it." She shook her head and willed herself to remain calm. Irrational behavior never helped anything. "Instead of feeling sorry for themselves, they enjoy life…thankful that they have 'that chair,' which enables them to not be shut in. And so can you. Why do you continue to be so obstinate? Why are you being so hard on yourself?" She couldn't jump him about being too prideful to use the chair. This went deeper than that and she knew it.

Instead of answering, he drove his chair to the window and stared out across the pasture.

"Don't you know how fortunate you are? You came through that plane crash alive. I understand it must have been a harrowing experience, but God brought you through it. What you have wrong with you can be fixed. I've tried and tried to get that through to you. You are about to be on a walker. And then a cane. But this is about more than walking, isn't it?" Instinct told her that Lacy was right. Wyatt was hiding something deeper. She could relate to that in more ways than he could imagine. Crazy as it sounded, she wished she could tell him her problem. But this was about him, not her, and it didn't seem right.

"Why are you so angry?" She asked the question half expecting him to scoff and tell her it was none of her business. Instead he swung his chair around to face her.

"Look, I took my life for granted, all right?" He rubbed his temple as if he had a headache.

"How did you do that?" It was the only question to ask to such an observation.

"I climbed into that plane never even imagining that it would crash. When I woke—" He stopped speaking and she stilled her fingers working out a knot tightening up along his spine. "When I woke trapped inside, with the smell of gas all around me, I felt stupid. I was going to die because I'd been incompetent. That isn't acceptable to me."

That couldn't be it. "You're this angry about being stuck in this wheelchair because you feel stupid?" This seemed totally out of character for him. She hadn't tagged him as being so shallow.

"No. Because like you just pointed out, I'm an arrogant fool."

"Hey, that's not what I meant at all!"

"Isn't it? It's the truth."

He was an overachiever. "Do you think you're a superhero? You're being unreasonably hard on yourself. You got in an airplane and it crashed. It happens. That's just like me getting in my car and being involved in that car crash—I didn't do it on purpose. I didn't drink and drive. *That* would be stupid. Was stupid, irresponsible and criminal."

He went very still. "You're right. But even if I weren't guilty of drinking…" His words were quiet. "I did know there was risk in taking off in that storm. All I can think about is what if I had harmed someone because I chose to fly my plane in unsafe conditions. I do corporate law for the most part, but I also handle cases every year where someone was injured from acts of neglect. It turns my stomach that I could have been in that category. At the very least I was neglectful of my own safety. My grandfather died that way. He basically made a decision to mow on a hill that any beginner would have known was too steep. But he did it anyway and his tractor rolled on top of him. All my life that's bothered me and here I went and decided to fly my plane into a storm because I believed I could fly through anything. God and everyone else has got to be thinking I'm an idiot. But that's not what bothers me. It's the carelessness of it. It's unforgivable."

There was a lot here. Amanda searched for words. "Everything is forgivable," she said. "I—I learned that when the drunk driver that had almost killed me came and begged me for forgiveness. I couldn't do it at first. But then, my dad helped me realize it was what God expected of me. He forgives us so we have to forgive others. It was tough at first. But that was the first step in my recovery. I've helped my young patients get through some of the same pain by helping them take that step. You need to do that. You need to forgive yourself." She walked over to stand beside him. She wanted to reach out and touch him but didn't.

He didn't look as if anything she'd said had made a difference. She pushed on. "You hold yourself up to too high a standard and you're right, that is pretty arrogant on your part. I hate to say this, but you don't have a clue what your grandfather was thinking." Maybe she was stepping over the line here, but she felt it needed to be said. Bluntness might be the only thing that got through to him.

He didn't say anything for a heartbeat. "You don't hold back, do you?"

"Not very often," she said, more gently. She wanted to help him. "I deal with people's physical impairments every day. Many times it's the things going on in their heads after an injury that play a role in their healing. My kids—I mean many of my patients—see counselors simultaneously. Normally, I leave this sort of thing for them."

"I don't know, you're giving this thick-headed fool sound advice. At least you are stating the facts."

"You deal in facts. I was probably out of line."

He lifted his hand and placed it on her arm. The contact was warm.

"You weren't out of line. I needed a kick in the pants. It's at least something for me to think about. New perspectives and all."

Her gaze was stuck on his hand on her arm. She forced herself to raise her head. "I hope if you think it's good advice, you'll take some of it. You aren't the type of man who would knowingly put yourself or someone else at risk. For some reason you were meant to be in this wheelchair in this moment in time."

"I don't know if I believe that."

He'd almost opened up a bit, but now he was shutting down again. Amanda pushed. "I don't begin to understand the mind of God. Believe me, I'm the worst—" She stopped herself. She could not go where she'd almost gone. "I believe that God has a reason and a purpose for everything. Whether you agree with him or not." If he only knew how hard it was for her to believe what she was saying. "Even you being in this wheelchair, at this time and place. Maybe it's so you'll go to church in this chair, and get over your pride—"

He shot her an icy glare. "Pride—" The phone rang and he reached for it. "I'm expecting a conference call. I'm not going to church."

And that was that. She watched him drive into the other room, frustration settling over her. He'd iced over like a freeze pop when she'd blurted out *pride*. Any moron would know you don't call someone on their pride unless you're prepared for them to cut you off instantly out of exactly that emotion.

She might not ever get him to listen to her now.

Chapter Nine

In the predawn hours of Sunday morning Wyatt gave up trying to sleep. He sat up, ignoring all the parts of him that protested with shooting pain. It wasn't his shoulder, his hip or his back or nightmares that kept him up for most of the night. It was Amanda.

She'd heaped the guilt on the day before. *Pride.* She'd thought he was too proud to be seen in the wheelchair. He hadn't needed her to point out to him that there were people who couldn't get out of their chairs. She'd acted like he didn't know this... He knew better than anyone that he could have very easily been one of them.

He carefully swung his legs over the edge of the bed, stood for a minute before easing into the wheelchair. He could feel the progress they'd made, feel the strength coming back to him and knew the pain was ebbing, also. Still, he despised the wheelchair more every day even knowing soon he wouldn't have to use it anymore.

He'd been whining.

He shouldn't have been startled by her boldness when she'd tried to put him in his place for it.

Whining. The thought hit him and it wasn't pleasant. The idea was so far removed from what he'd ever thought he'd do in the face of adversity that he wanted to shove it away and deny it.

Uncomfortable with the idea, he drove the chair to the kitchen and made himself a pot of coffee. By the time he poured himself a cup, he wasn't feeling any better about himself. He was still sitting at the front windows as the sun's morning light began to seep through the darkness. The last thing he was expecting to see as the thin sliver of pink crept over the treetops was Amanda. But there she was rounding the end of the house *jogging* down the road. But it was the prosthetic leg that caused him to almost drop his coffee.

She had on a blue top and gray running shorts that completely exposed the prosthetic leg made specially shaped for running. Her leg was missing from about five inches above the knee, and the prosthetic slipped over her thigh. The reality of what the drunk driver had done to her hit him like a punch in the gut, knocked the breath out of him. No wonder she'd given him a dressing-down over his attitude about the wheelchair. He felt sick. Even though he'd been in the process of taking a good hard look at himself, it didn't matter. Now he felt embarrassed by his entire attitude.

Here he was temporarily in a wheelchair with a clean bill of health ahead of him, according to Amanda and the doctors, and still he was whining.

Some man he turned out to be.

His disgust couldn't be measured, it was so great.

Amanda had lost her entire leg and hadn't said anything. No, on the contrary. She had taken what life had thrown at her and she'd triumphed over it. She'd become a physical therapist—working with kids who needed her attention and upbeat attitude. And on top of that she was running.

It was amazing.

He remembered her asking about his running and wondered why she'd chosen not to mention it then. Why had she not told him about her leg? *You fired her, you jerk, for being too small and too young.* She probably was afraid he'd fire her again if he knew about her leg. Remorse sank over him like a black cloud. She would have been right. For certain, he wouldn't have thought she was strong enough if he'd known this. He knew differently now, though. Amanda Hathaway was stronger than she looked…inside and outside.

Feeling like a fool, he watched her cross over the cattle guard and head down the gravel road dissecting the pastures. She followed the curved road across the prairie with such grace and fluidity that he found watching her hypnotizing.

Transfixed, he watched until she disappeared over the horizon where the trees peeked over the edge. He was profoundly and humbly changed as he sat there watching the spot where she'd disappeared.

Amanda had faced death and lost a limb and yet she'd overcome it. Instead of floundering as he'd been doing, she'd flourished.

Wyatt took a long draw on his coffee, then he turned his chair around and headed toward his bedroom.

Amanda pushed hard as she ran. Sleeplessness had driven her from her bed and out into the morning light with a vengeance. She'd given Wyatt all that advice the day before and felt like a hypocrite.

Why was it that depression and doubts always surged back just after progress was made? It was as if the devil were reaching out and pulling her back into the hole.

God had a reason and a purpose for everything.

Boy, she'd been real quick to spout that advice off to Wyatt. Even telling him that him being in that wheelchair at this time was His purpose—what had she been thinking? She didn't know God's reasoning. She kept trying to figure out her own way and couldn't do it, but she was sure full of advice for Wyatt.

So what had she been doing lecturing Wyatt on his attitude toward wheelchairs?

Needing to clear her head, she'd taken action, dressed in her running clothes, pulled on her running prosthetic and headed out into the gravel roads with the welcoming spirit she'd had all her life toward jogging. When she ran she was strong. She felt happy. She felt like anything was possible. And usually she felt at peace—that hadn't been the case for weeks. But still, she'd needed it these days more than ever.

"God never promised that life would always be easy," she said, out loud now. "He did promise that He would be with His people always and that He would help them. He will help Wyatt. And He will help me."

He would. It just seemed like...she couldn't find peace about it. Why was that? She felt such betrayal over what Jonathan had done, and she felt betrayed by God, too. This was where the turmoil lay.

She watched the sun rise as she ran down the gravel road that seemed to head straight for the glowing ball lifting upward. She asked God to give her the peace she needed....

If only she could get Jonathan and the life she'd envisioned with him off her mind.

And the children. Her purpose seemed so far away from her now she couldn't get her heart back into it.

She'd thought getting here to Mule Hollow and throwing herself into this job with a demanding client would be her saving grace. But this morning, the loss she felt inside was so great she could hardly stand it. All she could think about was never giving birth to her own children. Or having a husband.

"You *will* marry one day," she said, rather loudly. There was no one around to hear her and she needed to hear the words. "You will find a good man who won't think you aren't worth marrying because you can't carry his children…" Her voice broke and she stumbled to a stop; hands on her knees, she bent forward and blinked back the surge of tears that had risen suddenly. How was she supposed to help Wyatt when she couldn't help herself? Nothing she'd said the day before had gotten through to him.

The cattle kept on chewing as they studied her. It was like they were waiting for her to continue. *Focus.*

Amanda blinked hard and thought of

Wyatt. She was here to help him. "Suck it up and focus on what God has for you to do." Resuming her jogging, she evaluated her plan. Help him get on his feet. Help him get back to his life. Help him move past the things eating at him and holding him back. This job was about him, not her.

"You can help him."

And today that started with getting him to church. Getting him out of that house and back in the midst of people. She already knew that the folks of Mule Hollow would eagerly welcome him. She'd worry about herself later.

All she had to do was get him out of the house.

The last thing she expected an hour later, after she'd showered and dressed for church, was to round the corner to find Wyatt sitting on the porch with his Bible in his lap, also dressed for church.

She'd worried when she came back from jogging that he had seen her leg. She'd been so focused on running at the time that she'd overlooked the fact that he would be awake when she returned. But as she'd jogged past the house she'd decided if he was outside then it was meant to be. She was going to have to tell him anyway. It was time. He'd either respect her for the PT that she was or he'd give her the boot.

But finding him ready for church, in starched jeans and a crisp white shirt, threw her.

She halted at the bottom of the steps. "Hi. Don't you look nice." She didn't want to jump to conclusions, but her heart was pounding with hope.

His gaze was serious as he gave her a slow smile. "Thought I'd hitch a ride with you this morning, if that's all right."

A smile as wide as the Guadalupe River cracked across her face. "I think that would simply be wonderful."

The Mule Hollow Church of Faith was a sweet little number on the outskirts of town. The rural church made Amanda think of weddings and picnics on the lawn. The classic white-washed chapel with a tall steeple looked well maintained and inviting. It fit the country, down-home town perfectly and she could easily see happy couples standing together at the front of the church saying their vows before God and all of their friends and family. It would have been a lovely place for— *Hold it!* Amanda's thoughts came to a screeching halt. She was done imagining weddings. This was a good day and she didn't plan to spoil it. Wyatt had agreed to come to church with her and that had made her day brighter than she'd ever expected.

"I love it," she said, glancing at Wyatt. "Is this where you went to church growing up?"

"All my life. See that second window? I threw a baseball through that when I was nine. I thought my mother was going to kill me. She'd already told me that I needed to stop throwing the ball to Cole so close to the church because he might miss one. And he did. The ball tipped his glove and crashed through the window."

Amanda could just see them standing there. She knew without being told that Cole had idolized his big brother and Wyatt had probably taken his role as older brother seriously, even at that young age.

"You didn't listen," she guessed. His look said he'd been in hot water.

"You better believe I did the *next* time, though. I had to save up my own money to repay my parents for repairing the window. Plus, every Saturday for a month I had to weed the flower beds. I hated weeding then and more than ever now."

She laughed. "Your parents knew that, didn't they?"

"Oh, yeah. They got my attention."

Amanda laughed as she got out of the SUV. No sooner had she gotten the wheelchair unloaded from the chair rack on the back of the vehicle than they were spotted. Then surrounded. Poor Wyatt had more help getting out of the vehicle than he wanted, but he was pretty good at hiding his feelings. She, however, could tell that all the attention bothered him. She still didn't have a clue what had changed his mind, but she was glad they were here.

Norma Sue was the first to come barreling across the lawn with her husband, Roy Don, in tow. Wyatt filled her in on that tidbit as they came. The same with Esther Mae and her husband, Hank.

"It's a pure miracle that you got this man out of his house," Norma Sue said, practically tackling Wyatt to give him a hardy hug.

Esther Mae was right behind her. "We are so

glad you came," she said, pushing Norma Sue out of the way and getting her own hug. She had on a lime-green hat with red daisies clustered all about its brim, and when she engulfed Wyatt the brim whacked him in the nose.

"Like your hat, Esther Mae." He chuckled, meeting Amanda's gaze over Esther's shoulder. It looked as if his head was going to get squeezed right off.

"Don't smother him, Esther Mae," Norma Sue huffed.

"I'm not doing anything you didn't do," she snapped, finishing off with one more squeeze that caused the hem of her dress to dance right along with the daisies. "When do you get out of that?" she asked as she pulled away and straightened her hat.

It wasn't exactly the question Amanda had hoped Wyatt would get the minute he ventured out. She was afraid it wouldn't help the situation, but to her pleasant surprise, Wyatt didn't seem bothered. Instead he gave Esther Mae a gentle, almost flirtatious smile that had Amanda enjoying his interaction with the two older ladies.

"This next week is the goal, so says my boss." He gave Amanda a warm glance.

The charm in that glance and the way his voice dipped low on the last words sent a shiver of attraction racing through Amanda. Her heart lifted even more. Wyatt's sudden turnaround had given her own hard morning a turnaround. To her surprise, the sting of tears ambushed her. She looked down quickly and blinked them away. She'd been doing so well. Why now? Why were these emotions raging forward now, here? She could not cry in front of all these people.

Especially Wyatt.

She couldn't answer questions about what was wrong with her and she certainly didn't want Wyatt asking her what was wrong. Was it that her emotions were just so close to the surface that being happy for Wyatt's attitude adjustment was enough to set them off? That was all she could figure.

Wyatt caught sight of her staring and hiked a brow, ever so subtly. Immediately she realized that she'd been staring at him. She yanked her eyes from him and focused on what Norma Sue was saying.

"…your parents loved each other, too, and don't you ever forget it." Norma Sue patted his shoulder. "They'd be mighty proud of you."

Amanda couldn't help but look at him. His jaw jerked ever so slightly and he tensed up on his left side. As quick as that, he was suddenly in jeopardy of pushing himself into a spasm…all because something about that statement bothered him.

"Me and Esther Mae are singing the special in the choir this morning, so we have to head on in, too. See y'all later."

Esther Mae gaped at him, her big green eyes wide. "I still can't get over how great you look, Wyatt. Why, you're the picture of health." She grinned. "I think Amanda must be good for you." With that she spun and hurried after Norma Sue into the church.

Amanda's cheeks warmed.

"You know Esther Mae is right," Roy Don said, turning his attention on Wyatt as the ladies walked off. "If you were sitting in the pew and I didn't know any better I'd never a thought you couldn't walk—not saying you can't. But you know what I mean. It's a pure act of God Himself that you're sitting here. There's no doubt about it."

"Ain't that the truth," Hank agreed. "God don't just let everybody fall out of the sky and live to tell about it."

Wyatt's eyes darkened and he didn't look happy at all. Amanda braced for stormy weather.

"Well, fellas," he drawled. "You two sure know how to make a man feel good."

Both older men grinned. "We're glad we could help," Roy Don said. "Your daddy would want us to keep you knowing from where your blessings come."

"Yes, sir, he would," Wyatt said gruffly as they followed their wives into the church.

Amanda looked down at Wyatt as they went up the ramp. "Have you already thought about that?"

"You mean about how my dad would want me to know that God saved me for something?"

"Yes."

"Every single day since the crash," he said quietly, then drove through the doorway.

Chapter Ten

Babies. Meeting Lacy the day before should have prepared her for seeing other women who were expecting, but it didn't. There were pregnant women everywhere! Lacy gave both of them a big hug the minute they entered, then introduced Amanda to her husband, Clint. Obviously Clint and Wyatt knew each other well because they launched into a conversation immediately while Lacy began introducing her to the women as they passed by heading for their pews.

Thankfully there was so much going on that no one seemed to notice that she didn't ask the usual questions like "When are you due?" or "Is it going to be a boy or a girl?" She was able to smile, and she tried really hard to mean it. Meeting Lacy the day before she'd been able to focus on their conversation and not Lacy's pregnant state, but today it wasn't so easy. They were all so happy. She understood their joy completely.

She was relieved when Seth motioned to them from his pew to come join them.

"I never expected to turn around and see y'all here," he said, his disbelief apparent.

"Thought I'd see if I could shake things up a bit." Wyatt gave him a handshake.

Seth bent forward and grinned. "It's good to see you haven't lost your touch."

Amanda crowded into a pew next to Seth while Wyatt parked himself at the end of the pew. Melody, Susan and Cole all greeted them just as a cowboy stepped up to the mic and got the music started. From the choir Norma Sue and Esther Mae—surrounded by cowboys—smiled and she got the uncomfortable feeling they were grinning too big as their eyes kept going from her to Wyatt.

No sooner, it seemed, was the music over than the visiting preacher stood up and gave a sermon that ended almost before it had begun. The man told a joke—and not even a very good one—then he talked about an article he'd read in a popular magazine about some folks who'd done a good deed. Then it was over.

"We didn't pay him fer *that,* did we?" A tall, skinny, older man boomed in disgust as they were leaving. His thin face was rippled with frown lines.

Melody whispered to Amanda, "That's Applegate Thornton. He's hard of hearing and ornery but a total marshmallow. He's always looking out for Mule Hollow. I knew he wasn't going to be happy about this."

Seth stopped to talk. "Applegate, there's no need for you to get upset about this. I'm sure there are plenty of churches across the country who might like a five-minute sermon. We just aren't one of them."

"That's the surefire truth," a plump, balding man standing next to Applegate grumbled. "App, ole hypocrite, ya know good and well you got your moments when that'd be fine by you, too."

Melody leaned in close. "And that is Stanley Orr, Applegate's GBFF."

"What does that stand for?" she whispered. She could text message with the best of them, but those initials didn't compute to her.

Melody chuckled. "That stands for grumpy best friend forever. *Remember* I teach middle school."

Amanda bit back a laugh, totally picturing the two as "grumpy best friends forever"! While she and Melody were whispering, Applegate gave his GBFF a glare that would fry bacon it was so hot and a comeback—

"I ain't no *hypocrite!* Shor I might want ta go fishin' early ever once in a while, but I still expect a message. Even if it is a short one. That right thar was a touchy-feely piece of hogwash. That's what that was."

Amanda had to agree. There hadn't been one sincere thing in the sermon that spoke of being a word from God. But she wasn't worried about that, she was worried about the two old men as Seth, Cole and even Wyatt began to try and calm them down. "Are they okay?" she asked softly.

"Yes," Susan said, sidestepping the guys to stand beside Amanda and Melody. "They just get excited and they talk to each other like that all the time."

"They like to harass each other." Melody shook her head. "They can get pretty funny sometimes."

From behind her she heard Wyatt chuckle. It was a low rumble that made her want to smile. The sound of him chuckling and to see the way he'd relaxed were total reassurance that she'd done the right thing in trying to convince him to come to church. She still wasn't sure what had changed his mind, but she was giving all the credit to God.

"You hang around long enough and you'll see App and Stanley a lot. They're down at Sam's every morning playing checkers. They pretty much keep everyone in line and they can come up with some of the funniest things."

"Whatever you say. I'd have to see it to believe it," Amanda said. Her gaze was drawn to Wyatt. He was smiling and at ease as he got involved with the conversation. It was wonderful to see him this way. She was so glad he'd chosen to come with her.

Where had the man who'd been so adamant about not going to church in a wheelchair gone? This guy was the life of the party—and totally unknown to her.

"You've helped him already," Melody said about thirty minutes later.

She and Wyatt had gone back to Seth and

Melody's for lunch along with Cole and Susan. She was in the kitchen with Melody and Susan helping get lunch ready to serve.

Melody was a pretty brunette with violet eyes whose color and intelligence were accentuated by her purple glasses. Amanda could totally see her as the middle school history teacher that she was. "The fact that you got him to come to church in the wheelchair was amazing."

"And he actually smiled a couple of times," Susan said as she chopped tomatoes up for the salad. She was tall, blonde and beautiful—not at all what Amanda pictured as the local veterinarian when they'd met. But she was, and according to Wyatt her work was well-respected.

Amanda liked both women a lot. She still had a hard time looking at them and believing that one was married to a Turner brother and the other was about to be married to a Turner brother all because Wyatt had set them up. Wyatt Turner did not look like a cupid or a matchmaker. And he most definitely didn't look like a romantic, but that was exactly what he was in her eyes. She wondered why he didn't have a special woman in his life. Or maybe he did back in Dallas. What did she know?

Remembering the sound of his husky chuckle caused her pulse to skitter just thinking about it. That was a dangerous thing and she knew it. Today had been an awakening on many levels and she was seeing danger signals. The more he came out of his shell the more trouble she could have with these unwanted feelings of attraction.

"I've only been here this past week and a half, but I think he's doing better because he sees we are making progress." Eleven days she'd known Wyatt. It seemed longer. "I'm surprising him tomorrow with a walker."

"Oh, Seth is going to be ecstatic," Melody gasped.

"Cole, too. Oh, Amanda, you are amazing," Susan said. "I'm telling you, getting him out of that chair is going to bring out a whole new side to him. If you think the change over the last few days is something, this is going to blow you away."

Amanda could believe that. She already was, truth be told.

Chapter Eleven

Wyatt studied Amanda as she drove them back home. He was glad he'd gone to church. But he'd been thinking about Amanda most of the time. Maybe what she said about God having a reason for placing him in this chair was true. Maybe. But how did she view the fact that she'd lost her leg? Had this been the reason her fiancé had broken off their engagement? The idea had hit him not long after she'd jogged past him. It had plagued him all through church, when he had to pretend to everyone that he was great—he was great from the standpoint of what she'd done for his physical therapy. But from the standpoint of how he'd behaved from day one of meeting Amanda until now, he was about as shamed as a man could get. And he had been trying to figure out the best way of going about giving her an apology.

"Why didn't you tell me about your leg?" Not exactly tactful but it got things moving. It wasn't as if he could get any more sorry than she probably already thought he was.

She turned her head. "You saw me this morning?"

"If you don't want to talk about it I understand…." He paused and decided to open up and lay it on the line. "But, look, I owe you. I needed everything you threw at me yesterday. And today was good for me. I'm glad you opened my eyes and got me there in this wheelchair. It was a good perspective for me to see. I don't know why you haven't told me about your leg, but I can make an educated guess."

She looked at him apologetically. "I meant to tell you. But you'd already fired me once for looking too young. I didn't think my having only one leg would give you any confidence in me."

They crossed the cattle guard and stopped in front of the house. She didn't have to say that she'd thought he'd look at her handicap as a negative. He felt sick. "Honestly, I probably would have done that then. But now that I've seen you in action, I'm sorry. I shouldn't have been thinking that either way. But I can't change it. All I can do is tell you I'm sorry now."

"I feel like I should have said something. Don't apologize."

He touched her arm. "Amanda, I'm about to get out of this chair because of you and I'm grateful for all you're doing for me—I owe you that since I haven't been the best patient. You weren't the only one. My brothers knew, besides. It was on your résumé."

She looked as if she hated admitting this even more. "Yes. But I assumed they were waiting on me."

"I said something to them. They told me they didn't want to give me any other reason not to let you stay. So they kept quiet. They laughed and said it was my fault for being so pigheaded. I have to agree."

"I've had tougher, believe me."

It was his turn to be skeptical. "No kidding?"

"Kids can be tough when they are adjusting to loss of a limb. I understood." She turned the ignition off and their eyes held.

The silence cocooned them in the vehicle and Wyatt felt transfixed by the understanding and forgiveness in her eyes. "You're a good woman, Amanda." He was startled when her eyes suddenly grew bright with tears. He reacted by reaching to touch her arm again, but she blinked hard, opened her door and was gone. He got out slowly and waited while she unloaded the motorized wheelchair from the ramp. He told himself to remember this was strictly a business relationship and he would not cross the line.

"I think you'll be happy to know that this is your last ride in this thing," she said, too brightly. "You are moving on to the next step as soon as you drive into the house. Starting then, you will be on your walker."

"That's great." He figured he should have been elated. But all he could think about as he drove up the ramp and into the house was Amanda and what she was hiding behind that too-bright smile of hers. Why had she almost cried when he told her she was a good woman? Did she think she wasn't?

Did she think the engagement ending

meant she wasn't a good woman? Questions swirled in his brain.

Had she been told she wasn't?

He wheeled the chair around, ready to ask and find out. *Strictly business, cowboy,* the voice in his head warned.

She glanced at him and immediately disappeared inside the workout room. When she returned a few moments later she carried the walker over and set it down in front of him.

"Let's try this out."

He stared up at her, contemplating the right move.

"Well, don't look so excited," she said. Her serious eyes seemed to beseech him not to continue with where his thoughts were going…he'd seen that look before. From people who'd sworn to tell the truth and had just realized they were about to be asked questions that would pry into an area of their life they didn't want to talk about.

"It's time to stand up, Wyatt. Stand up and let's park that scooter."

"You're right." She didn't want to talk about her personal life and had come here for a job to escape talking and thinking about her breakup. Wyatt reminded himself that he was her work. Not her friend or her keeper. He was her client.

And he'd do well to remember that.

There was an uneasy tension between them. It ran just beneath the surface of their cordiality, as if she was afraid if he studied her hard enough he'd see all the way through her.

It made her uncomfortable.

"That's as far as it will go," Wyatt said on Thursday morning. It had been four days since he'd started using the walker.

She smiled encouragement. "Don't worry, you're coming along great. Okay, stand and do the weights." She watched him stand up. He was growing stronger by the day. She handed him the five-pound weights he would use to strengthen the rotator cuff and stabilize it.

"How did you sleep last night?" she asked, watching as he held the weight in his hand, kept his arm close to his body, elbow tucked in at his side, and then swept the weight out and away from his body. She touched his elbow to make sure he kept it motionless. "That's good." She watched him do his repetitions. "Sleep?" she asked when he'd set the weights down and turned toward her. Weariness met her eyes as she looked up at him.

"Rough," he admitted. "But that's nothing new. This thing is just uncomfortable as all get-out at night."

"Are you placing the pillows like I showed you?"

"Yes, it's helped some." He was staring down at her, searching her eyes. It felt personal. She was so close to him that she felt the heat of his arm against hers. Her mouth went dry and her pulse quickened. This was trouble. He was her patient—racing pulses were totally off-limits. Bottomless stomachs and breathlessness were, too. She backed up—so quickly she ran into the weight rack. It wobbled and she stumbled as she reached down to steady it, but Wyatt's hand closed securely around her arm.

"Easy there. We don't need you falling and hurting yourself." His blue eyes bored into hers before dropping to her mouth. "We would be in a mess, both hobbling around here."

Her skin burned—of course it did—where his fingers closed around her arm. She couldn't have formed a coherent sentence to save her life. All she could do was nod up at him.

"You don't sleep much yourself." His voice was as smooth as his hand was steady. His gaze lifted back to hers.

"What do you mean?"

"The jogging at sunrise, that's what."

She smiled tightly. "It's something I love to do. No big deal."

"No big deal. You and I both know you running is a big deal for you—and impressive. You're gone hours."

He'd really been watching her. The thought pleased her more than she could have known. "Why have you been paying so much attention?"

His lips curved gently and he dipped his chin as if talking to a child. "Amanda, I pay attention because you're alone in my pasture in the wee hours of the morning. I worry about you. I like to know you get back safely."

"I'm safe." Amanda took a breath and tried to calm the butterflies rolling around in her stomach as disappointment washed over her—he was concerned because she was on his property.

For a moment she'd thought—*hold it,*

sister, just one minute there—what had she thought? That he was watching out of concern for her because he *cared?*

The very idea sent her into a tailspin. Yes, she was attracted to Wyatt like she'd never been attracted to anyone…not even Jonathan. But she'd just been engaged— dumped didn't matter—she'd been engaged and now she was seriously having thoughts of another man this soon after thinking she'd been in love. What kind of woman did that make her?'

No, Wyatt was wonderful, handsome, built like a dream and deserved better than she could give him—so why was she even thinking about that? Besides, she knew now that she could never risk being rejected again. She needed to keep her head on straight and remember this was a patient/client relationship and would never be anything more.

"You're doing good with this exercise," she said. "You're building strength, and you should be feeling relief soon. Like I tell my kids, no matter what you do, keeping good muscle tone is the secret key."

"I'm not complaining." He continued with

his exercise, slowly going through different sets of exercises she'd shown him.

"So the kids you worked with were mostly amputees like you?" Wyatt asked after a few repetitions.

"Yes. I loved working—I mean, I used to enjoy working with the kids because they'd been through so much and it was an awesome feeling to be able to ease some of their fears of the unknown and also prepare them for life after their loss."

"I bet that was rewarding." He paused and studied her.

What did she say to that? It had been rewarding until the reality hit her that she could never have her own children. "It was. I didn't like it when insurance coverage ran out and I had to leave before I felt like they were ready."

He set the weights down and eased into the cane-backed chair at the table. "Did that happen a lot?"

She huffed with frustration. "Too often. Amputees—uninsured and insured alike—have a hard time with the expense of prosthetics. I've always wished I could do more. But I haven't figured out how to do that. I could only give them as much help as I could in the time I was there and leave them with an in-depth plan of action for when I was gone. That and my phone number in case they had any questions. It seems to work fairly well."

"You sound really dedicated. I'm amazed you decided to move to working with adults. Sounds like those kids really need you out there showing them the way."

Why had she even let this conversation get started? Her mouth was dry as she tried to look unshaken by his words.

"There was a lot of stress. I've been comfortable with the decision I made."

His gaze seemed to sharpen as he studied her with piercing eyes.

"What are you not saying?"

She stood up and glanced at her watch. The session was over. "I'm not saying anything except that you did a great job today and should be proud. You did great on your walking exercises, too. Keep it up and before you know it I'll be handing you a cane."

The expression on his face told her that he wasn't fooled by her. "Sounds like a plan," he said, much to her relief.

She would eventually grow more at ease

talking about this. Surely the pain she felt about losing her ability to carry a child would ease. At least to where she could function and have a conversation about it.

"My back and hip are feeling better every day, I have to admit," Wyatt said a week later. He was practically giving himself a pep talk! She was proud of him.

"And you are using a cane. Don't forget that."

"That is correct," he said in that way of his as he held up the cane. "Thanks to you, I'm almost a brand-new man."

His smile was a dazzler and sent butterflies fluttering inside Amanda. "That's good to hear," she croaked, trying to ignore the growing attraction and feelings toward him. "H-how about your shoulder? Start your exercise and tell me how it feels today." She zeroed in on his shoulder and avoided his gaze. He placed his pointer finger and index finger on the wall like she'd shown him. Starting at shoulder level, he slowly walked them upward along the wall. His shoulder extension was improving incrementally.

She watched as he did the exercise again.

She still couldn't believe the change in him since Sunday a week ago. "Good," she said. "This time continue higher if you can."

He nodded and concentrated hard on extending his arm higher.

Ever since he'd found out about her amputation, he'd been different. He worked hard, complained less and was easier to get along with. He'd told her what she'd said had done him good. That he'd needed to hear it. But she could also tell that he felt remorse about her leg as if he felt guilty he'd complained.

They'd been working hard. Wyatt wanted to be ready for Cole's wedding, but it also seemed that he worked hard to please her— or maybe to make her feel better. It was almost as if he didn't want her to feel like he was taking her for granted. Why she got that feeling she wasn't sure—maybe it was because he'd been so careful to thank her. So careful not to complain.

Even so, that hadn't stopped him from trying to find out more about her. As if he wanted her to talk about Jonathan…as if he thought talking might help her. And it had almost worked several times—he was an expert at leading the conversation toward her. She could see where this uncanny ability of his would come in handy in his career choice. But she had been equally determined to not go there if at all possible. She was struggling as it was with finding her footing, and so she'd led all conversations right back to something general.

Each time, he'd backed off with a small smile. A smile that told her he knew she was evading him. It was a challenge not to let herself spill her every troubled heartache to him.

"You've been working overtime," he said, drawing her thoughts back to the moment. "But I've been behaving and doing just what the doctor ordered."

She gave him a thumbs-up. "Yes, you have. Now let's see you walk across the room with just this cane. Take it slow. We are pressing things a bit, but I know you can do it."

He started walking, his steps halting.

"When will I stop dragging this foot?"

"We'll have you with a normal gait soon. But not before the wedding, I'm afraid. You'll be able to stand and walk, but you won't be at a hundred percent. Right now, you just concentrate on your steps. How does your back feel?"

He made it slowly, carefully across the room and sank heavily down into the chair beside her.

"How can that exhaust me?" he growled, his brows dipping in consternation. His shoulder rested against hers and it took all her willpower not to lean into him. Especially when he was staring at her, so close she could see the tiny light blue specks that dotted the dark blue of his eyes. Her stomach fluttered again and she breathed steady, trying to make herself get straight.

Her defenses were down today. The emotions that she'd locked inside her heart threatened to overwhelm her suddenly. She'd dreamed of children all night long—children she would never give birth to. She'd awakened near tears and longing for comfort…all she could think about was how it would be to feel Wyatt's arms around her. It grew harder each day she spent around him. And now this—she didn't need to go there.

"Talking does help, you know."

Amanda hadn't meant to get lost in her thoughts. She shook her head, so tempted to talk to him that she didn't trust herself. "Not for me. I'm sorry, Wyatt, I need to go."

She hurried to the door.

"Amanda!" Wyatt's call followed her but she didn't look back. No, she was too intent on putting as much space between them as possible.

As she fled the stagecoach house, the need to talk to him was like nothing she'd ever experienced before. As gruff and ill-tempered as Wyatt had been, she knew that he would listen to her with a compassionate ear.

If she threw herself into his arms—which she might have done seconds later if she hadn't fled the premises—he would hold her and comfort her, because that was the kind of man he was.

Once at the trailer, she slammed the door and locked it. As if that would keep her from turning around and going back!

Closing her eyes, she inhaled slowly, trying to calm her racing heart.

She was mixed up about her entire state of mind. She needed to talk to someone. Her gaze landed on the Bible as if drawn there, like it had been the last time she'd come up with no answers. She felt a need to try reaching out to God once more. She needed to know what her purpose was. Surely He had a plan for her and all the things that she'd been through. There had to be reasons for the way her life was turning out.

What are Your plans for me? There had to be a reason she was left to feel such emptiness.

Her knees were weak as she stared at the Bible.

She'd been reading it and searching it and nothing had helped yet. It was as if God was trying to get her attention, but she simply couldn't find what He was trying to get her to see.

What kind of person had she become?

God didn't want her to feel this way. Her mind knew this. Her heart knew this. But deep inside none of that helped.

So why did she think Wyatt could make anything better?

Chapter Twelve

"You raised all of this?" Amanda asked Melody a couple of days after her meltdown. Melody had called and asked if she would like to see her vegetable garden and then go with her into town to help plan the wedding with some of the other ladies. Amanda jumped at the chance to get out of the house, though she worried it might trigger another meltdown. But she needed out and away from Wyatt. They were dancing around each other like two eighth graders at their first dance. She continued to want to find comfort in his arms, but she wasn't kidding herself, either. She knew there was more to it than that.

Melody smiled and pushed her purple glasses firmly into place in front of her shining violet eyes. "I can't take all the credit. Poor Seth." She shook her head in sympathy for him. "I worked him to death getting him to help me prepare the soil out here."

"It's *huge*." Amanda laughed in amazement. "This is half a football field! You could feed an army."

Melody put her hands on her hips and proudly surveyed her living masterpiece. "It's only about a half acre. I still have tomatoes, though the drought has made it tough this month. August is dry anyway, but without rain it's a chore. I had corn but now I'm doing peas and beans. Over there I've got watermelons and cantaloupe. And all kinds of peppers—I honestly don't know what I'm going to do with all the salsa I'm going to make." She handed Amanda a basket. "Come on. Pick all you want. Seth and I have to go out to the other ranch the family owns on Friday and I'm not sure how much of this will still be alive when I get back. But this might be my last time for a little while to go with him since I'll be starting back to school next week."

"Do you need me to do something while

you're gone?" Amanda asked, picking a tomato.

"Well, the ranch hands are supposed to water, but I just worry that it won't be done like I want it done." They were walking down opposite sides of the row of tomatoes. Melody looked around a huge plant with a sheepish look on her face. "I really don't mean that to sound rude. It's just they are cowboys, not farmers. Even if my Seth was in charge of it I would be worried. They're thinking about cattle."

Amanda plucked a plump, juicy tomato. The color was deep orange and she knew from the ones she'd eaten at Melody's it would taste just as great as it looked. "I've got time on my hands during the day. I'd love to come and take care of this for you." Boy, would she.

"Are you sure?"

"Yes," Amanda said. "I don't know much about gardens, but I really want to do this. I'm close and there's no need for you to make your cowboys be farmers."

"Is Wyatt driving you that crazy?"

"No. Well, a little. But not in a bad way. I mean…" Amanda couldn't blame this all on Wyatt. "I have some things on my mind.

Things that happened before I came here. I really could use something to occupy my mind and hands."

Melody stopped picking tomatoes and real concern etched her face. "Is it something I can help with?"

"No—"

"Is it another man?"

Amanda shook her head too vehemently.

"It *is*," Melody gasped, her eyes tender. "You have a boyfriend?"

"No," Amanda said. "I *had* a fiancé." There, she'd been honest about it. What did it matter anyway? Really. She needed to move on and she saw in telling Wyatt that it was okay.

"You were getting married. Does Wyatt know this?"

"I told him the other day."

"I'm glad you were able to confide that in him. I don't mean to pry, but how are you?"

"I'm *better* than I was. I've struggled, but I am thankful that it ended before we said our vows."

"That is a blessing. You need the man God has waiting for you. I know this has to hurt, but God will send the right man—maybe sooner than you want." She smiled sheepishly. "Who knows what the future holds? Look at the witness your life is since losing your leg. That is testimony to your strength right there."

Amanda went back to picking vegetables. "That's what I want it to be." They'd reached only halfway down the row but already her basket was overflowing with tomatoes. "I can't carry anything else in this basket." She laughed, staring at the abundance of those left. This garden would keep the entire town supplied. Why in the world had Melody planted so many plants? "What's going to happen to all of these?"

"Oh, don't worry about that. I've invited the ladies from No Place Like Home out to pick whatever they want. That's the women's shelter that Dottie and Brady Cannon run. Brady is our Sheriff."

"I didn't know there was a women's shelter here."

"It's been here for a couple of years. You know the candy store in town? That's run by the ladies. Dottie teaches them candy making and how to run a business while they are at the shelter. It is really a wonderful ministry."

"It sounds like it."

"And Wyatt wouldn't tell you this, but he does all the legal stuff for the ladies if they need it. And he does it for free."

"He does?" She hadn't meant to sound so shocked. And she really wasn't; she'd already figured out that he was a good man.

Melody eyes twinkled with merriment. "He truly is a nice guy. We weren't just saying that. He does stuff like that all the time."

"I've figured that out about him. He's been out of his element."

"Like we told you the other day, we were all so worried about him after the crash. I don't know if you've caught on to the fact that he thinks he is everyone's keeper. You see, Seth told me that after their parents died, even though Wyatt was only a senior in high school he took on the role of being the head of the house. He feels responsible for Seth and Cole. Even so, they want him to think about himself now. They'd hoped that he would come back here someday and settle down. He got Cole home, now they'd like him here, too. But that may never happen."

Amanda listened with interest. They'd

walked back to the front of the garden and Melody set her basket down and she did the same. She took a small basket when Melody handed it to her.

"Let's grab some peppers before the poor bushes fall over under the weight."

Amanda was thinking about Wyatt as they walked over to the peppers. Her perspective of Wyatt was very muddled. What she'd just learned explained more about his frame of mind. He'd taken on responsibilities of a grown man at an early age. He was probably an overachiever prior to that, but the responsibility of his brothers and the ranch had probably made him more so. No wonder he'd been so hard on himself. He'd not been irresponsible ever, it seemed. Not until he got into that plane and took off in that storm.

She was only twenty-four, but she knew that what she'd gone through at fourteen had aged her beyond her years. Her respect for Wyatt went up knowing this about him. There was absolutely no denying that he was one of the good guys. One of the really good men of Mule Hollow.

"You know, some woman is going to really be blessed when Wyatt falls in love with her,"

Melody said. Her pretty eyes blinked innocently from behind her glasses.

Amanda felt uncomfortable suddenly at what Melody was hinting. "So, there isn't anyone special in his life right now?" Amanda had no business asking, but the question just kind of came out.

Melody shook her head as she twisted a red bell pepper from the bush. "Never has been, according to Seth. Wyatt works. He dates, don't get me wrong, but he's not been interested in marriage. That's one of the things that has been so curious about him being so determined to find Cole and Seth wives. He just felt like that was his responsibility, to get them married and happy. Funny how he associates happiness with marriage. I think deep down inside he wants the same thing for himself. He just hadn't slowed down from his career long enough to remember that there is life beyond the law practice."

"That is for certain. The man never stops. He brought the practice home with him." She and Melody paused on that, perplexed.

Melody shook her head. "Cole and Susan had decided to go ahead with the wedding Saturday after next since Wyatt is on a cane now. They are so happy and anxious to be married. Cole is going to go by today and tell Wyatt. We're hoping that as soon as they're married that maybe Wyatt will be next."

Amanda wasn't sure what to make of Melody's wistful smile. "Maybe so," she said. "I'm sure back in Dallas there are plenty of women who would want that spot in his heart. And fit into his lifestyle."

"Like I said, we're praying he'll fall in love with a Mule Hollow girl."

"Well, good luck with that." Amanda hated to discourage Melody, but she didn't see that happening ever. Wyatt Turner might be a cowboy at heart, but she didn't see a country girl fitting into his life at all. His heart was in Dallas. Why else would he be consulting on all these cases?

He obviously couldn't wait to get back to it…and besides, though they didn't know it, she knew clearly that she wasn't the right woman for any man.

Wyatt stared at the floor through the face-hole in the massage table and tried hard to keep his mouth shut. It was obvious Amanda had no desire whatsoever to talk about herself. It was driving him crazy. The last few days had been like a bad rodeo. He'd try to talk to her and she'd shut him out. He felt like he'd been bucked off straight out of the chute at every turn.

Not only was he concerned about her, but he was finding himself more and more attracted to her. It was so bad lately that even when he was supposed to be working he was thinking about her.

And he couldn't stop wondering about that deep sadness he'd kept glimpsing. What made her sad? Had she loved this man so much she couldn't forget him? Couldn't move forward? What was it?

Staring at the floor, he fought wanting to press her. If he started questioning her he was afraid it would come out sounding like an interrogation.

Amanda Hathaway was a mystery to him. He didn't like mysteries until they were solved.

What he knew was that he'd misjudged her in the worst way the day she'd arrived. She'd told him she was good and that she'd have him back to new if he only trusted her. She was holding up her end of the challenge with ease. Even with her disability.

Yes, he was attracted to her, but more important he respected her—and it took a lot to win his respect. And she was completely immune to him in every way.

It was downright depressing.

Oh, she'd had him thinking a few days ago when she'd stumbled over the weight rack that maybe she was attracted to him. When he'd touched her he'd *almost* made a fool of himself and tried to kiss her. No way did he need to start thinking about that again. It was ridiculous. He was a thirty-six-year-old man and she had him feeling like a mixed-up schoolboy.

"You need to relax," she demanded, pressing hard on the muscles lining his spine. "You're so knotted up that you're going to seize up on me."

"This is as good as it gets," he growled. If she thought he was going to relax today, she was dreaming.

"In that case, I'm just spinning my wheels."

He felt her draw back from him and then her footsteps headed away from him. He yanked his head up, staring over his shoulder as she disappeared down the hall. "Hey, you're not through."

"I am today," she called from the kitchen.

Using his good arm he eased up to a sitting position and then got off the table, wincing when he moved too quickly. This was getting old despite the progress he'd made. He didn't feel a hundred years old anymore, but he was still pushing eighty.

"Why did you walk off like that?" he demanded as he eased into the kitchen. "You are real good at walking away."

She was chopping up peppers and her back was to him. Her short hair swung about her ears to the very aggressive rhythm of the knife. At his accusation she glared at him.

He'd been surprised to find out that she was a good cook. She'd been thrilled with all the things she'd been getting from Melody's garden earlier that week and he'd been benefiting from it. Her early morning omelettes made his mouth water. But good cook or professional cook, she was being far too scary with that knife at the moment.

What was she thinking? Her gaze shot back to her task. Angry, he stalked over—as best he could given his gait—and leaned against the counter next to the eggs and mixing bowl she'd set out. His hip ached and his back throbbed, but none of that bothered him more than the fact that she was hiding something important from him and he wanted to know what it was. Maybe it was the lawyer in him that wanted to always dig deep to find the truth, and the why of what made people do things. Until you knew the whole story, you couldn't find the right solution.

But he knew that wasn't it where Amanda was concerned. It was the man in him that simply wanted to know what was bothering the woman he was beginning to care about. The knowledge had its problems, but at the moment he wasn't thinking about them.

"You're going to cut your fingers off if you keep that up."

"I can handle this," she snapped.

That did it. "Not on my watch." He reached for the knife. "Give me the knife."

"No." Icy eyes glared at him, but she stopped chopping. A good thing.

"I said—hand over the knife. I'm not playing with you, Amanda. I'm in the mood for breakfast at Sam's this morning."

"Well, I'm not."

"Doesn't matter. I am and you're going to

drive me. It's your *job*. Or did you forget?"
He wasn't playing fair, but he didn't care.

She stared at him like he had just lost his
mind. Maybe he had. All he knew was he
was taking her out to breakfast—in a weird
roundabout way.

"I'm not going to be good company."

"Fine. There will be plenty of good
company to be had even if you choose to sit
in the corner and pout. Now hand over the
knife."

Pout! Wyatt thought she was pouting. She
handed him the knife. She'd been struggling
to not fall for Wyatt but it was happening
despite everything she was doing.

"Thank you very much." He took the knife
and dropped it into the sink. "Let's go."

She had no choice but to follow him out
to the SUV.

The whole way into town, the tension
between them escalated…even though they
didn't say much. Maddening as it was, he
seemed relaxed, which made her all the more
tense. She was trying to keep her distance
from him, but with every piece of new information about him everyone was so keen on

throwing her way it was almost impossible. And then there was the issue of him pressing her to find out what was bothering her. The man was relentless.

"You're in for a treat if you haven't had Sam's breakfast."

He didn't sound mad or upset, even though he'd forced her to come along. He sounded like he was looking forward to spending time with her—dangerous.

Maybe if he'd been talking to her, she wouldn't have been *thinking* about how good he looked…or how he'd gotten under her skin in the few short weeks since she'd known him.

What she needed was for him to go back to being Mr. Ill-Tempered and make it impossible to like him, or worse, for her to…to be thinking fairy-tale thoughts about what falling in love with him would be like.

"I'm not much of a breakfast eater," she said, fighting to fill the holes that were being blown into the barrier around her heart. But oh, what did Wyatt do? He grinned! And it was no small grin. No, this was a wickedly fun grin, that sent mischief to his eyes and an electric shock to her like she'd been hit with a Taser.

"You are determined to be miserable, aren't you?" he asked, still smiling. Totally enjoying himself!

"I'm only telling the truth," she snapped. *Now* she sounded like a child pouting!

The amused twinkle in his eyes said he thought the same thing as he opened the door and got out.

With his weak arm, a bad hip, a bad back and a cane to maneuver with, he needed to be more careful. *"Wait!"* she exclaimed. Jumping from the SUV, she hurried around to help him, fearful that he might fall—and she'd have to catch him!

He was standing beside the open door watching her, still grinning. "You could have hurt yourself," she snapped, closing the door with a snap.

"I figured that was the way to get you out of the truck for breakfast."

She shot daggers at him. "You are not playing fair."

"Never said anything about playing fair. One thing you need to know about me is I do what I need to do—"

"Okay, okay, I'll eat breakfast. But I'm warning you, buster, I can play dirty, too."

That got her a deep, baritone laugh that made her knees weak. As she followed him up the steps she had a feeling she was in for a rough ride. This Wyatt Turner, the playful one, might possibly be irresistible.

Chapter Thirteen

❧

"Stanley, would ya look at that," Applegate said, jumping his red checker as he scrunched busy eyebrows together and stared at Amanda and Wyatt entering the diner.

They were sitting at the front window table with a checkerboard between them. There was a five-pound bag of sunflower seeds sitting beside them and on the floor at Stanley's feet was a brass spittoon.

Staring wide-eyed at them, Stanley spit in rapid-fire succession and the shells hit the spittoon's mouth dead center. "Wyatt, yor walkin'. That's a real sight fer sore eyes. I almost didn't turn around and look cuz I figured ole App was tryin' ta pull a slick one on me."

"Are you saying App here cheats?" Wyatt asked as he walked slowly toward them.

Stanley tugged at his ear. "Naw, he don't. But if he wants ta beat me, he's gonna have ta start."

Applegate frowned and cut his eyes at his buddy. "Don't believe it. I beat him plenty. Might be doin' it right now if he don't watch out."

Despite her qualms about coming, Amanda had to smile at the two friends. She was distracted, though, by the breakfast scents emanating from the kitchen. Goodness, but the place smelled great.

"Well, look what the cat dragged up." Sam hustled out of the kitchen. "It's about time you came in and brought this little gal with you. Leave them two ornery coots alone and let's get this little gal a booth."

Applegate grinned, his lean face a cascade of wrinkles. "Y'all jest have a seat over thar while I beat the socks off of Stanley here."

Sam was waiting at the booth all the way across the diner from App and Stanley, and Wyatt led the way to it.

"This is great, Sam." Wyatt remained standing while she took her seat. There was absolutely nothing romantic about eating breakfast in an old-fashioned diner with three old men watching, but Amanda still got butterflies as Wyatt slid carefully into the seat across from her.

She had to get over this. She had to—had to—had to!

"How you doin', Amanda? Keepin' this fella straight?" Sam set two mugs on the table in front of them.

"I'm trying." She nodded when Sam lifted the pot so she could indicate whether she wanted him to fill her mug.

Applegate grunted loudly from across the room. "That ain't never been an easy task."

Amanda thought he had a problem with his hearing.

"It's good to see you out of that wheelchair. That jest didn't look right."

"It shor didn't," Stanley boomed, spitting a sunflower seed into the spittoon. "Growing up, this fella never stopped. Always workin' with his grandpa or his daddy. Or later, with them brothers and on that ranch. Your folks would be proud of you, son."

"Thank you, sir. That means a lot to me." Knowing what she did about him now,

Amanda knew this did mean the world to Wyatt. It was apparent that everything he'd done had been to make them proud and to fill the gap their deaths had made in his brothers' lives.

"Now, though, you need ta get yourself home where you belong." Sam set the pot on the burner and Applegate's face fell into a river of wrinkles. "It jest ain't right, you bein' away like you are. Yor a Turner. Turner men belong here."

Wyatt shrugged his good shoulder. "I've been through this with y'all a hundred times. I'm good at what I do. I'm happy in Dallas."

Sam, Applegate and Stanley all shook their heads. Amanda watched, fascinated. These men were serious. They wanted Wyatt home as much as Seth and Cole. *Everyone* wanted him home. But it was obvious that Wyatt didn't want it.

"What would y'all like ta eat?" Sam grumbled. "Ain't no way yor gettin' my kinda cookin' over yonder in that city."

Stanley jumped a checker and grinned at Applegate's scowl. "Yeah, you used ta tell Sam he was the best cook in the world when you was knee-high to a grasshopper and yor grandpa would sit you up thar on that bar stool on a stack of *The Farmers' Almanacs*."

"Sam's food *is* the best. I never disputed that. Why do you think I made my lovely physical therapist bring me here as soon as I got this cane? I want my usual, Sam. How about you, Amanda?"

He'd called her *lovely*. Of course he was teasing the older men, but his eyes warmed her blood as they settled on her. Electricity seemed to hum in the air. She grabbed the plastic menu from beside the silver napkin holder and stared at the breakfast menu. A visual of Wyatt as a child sitting at the bar with his grandpa played across her mind's eye. He would have been a cute little kid. Inquisitive and probably bossy. No probably about it, he would have been bossy. He'd have been a take-the-world-by-the-horns child straight from the womb, she was pretty certain. His children would no doubt be the same.

She met his gaze and he had a mischievous light in his eyes as he watched her. Almost as if he could read her thoughts. The man would probably have been a great poker player—they did say he took after his many-greats Grandpa Oakley who'd won the stage-coach house in a poker game. "I'll have the Texas French Toast," she blurted, only because it was the first thing on the menu. Wyatt's grin lifted crookedly—and she was certain he was looking inside her head and figuring everything out. She swallowed the lump that lodged in her throat and found herself unable to look away.

"How did you do that?" Applegate snapped, his voice breaking the spell like a bullhorn.

Amanda cut her eyes to the checker players and saw he was glaring at the board.

Stanley looked smugly at her. "I pert near get him every time. And he never learns. He was too busy watching you two make goo-goo eyes at each other to see he'd left me a three-jump opening."

"Goo-goo eyes!" Amanda exclaimed before she caught herself. "I was not doing any such thing."

"Yup. That's what I saw. And I'm glad ta see it."

She stared at Applegate and slammed her mouth shut or she might have said something she would regret. She regretted this breakfast, that was a given. And Wyatt wasn't helping. Oh, no, he was laughing. His shoulders were hunched over he was laughing so hard. *Shaking.* His shoulders were shaking with his laughter. This was ridiculous.

"I do not, have never and will not ever make goo-goo eyes at my patients."

"Well, we certainly hope not." Stanley chuckled right along with Wyatt. "If ya did that, then what would be special about you and our boy here ogling each other? Nothin', that's what."

Amanda was going to be sick. She hadn't meant to get this sort of talk started. She hadn't meant to stare at Wyatt like a lovesick puppy right here in front of everyone. But who would have thought three crusty old men—two who were sitting across the room—would start talking about goo-goo eyes. Wyatt didn't look any happier than she was.

"Hey, fellas, hold off on marrying me and Amanda off. For one, she's way too young for me. For two, I'm not on the market and for three, Amanda doesn't like me much."

Amanda couldn't believe he'd just come out and said that in front of everyone. Too young. That one really got her. The man thought she was too young. There were only twelve years' difference in them. "I like you," she hissed, leaning toward him across the table. "Just not like that. Besides, fellas, I'm not looking for a husband right now."

Sam came out and set her steaming plate of French toast down in front of her. He grinned as he slid Wyatt's bacon and eggs in front of him. "And why not?" Sam looked insulted on Wyatt's behalf.

"Yeah," Stanley joined in. He had abandoned the checker game and was digging a handful of sunflower seeds. "He's handsome, funny—"

"And," App broke in, "he's got a highfalutin job and owns a bunch of land."

At that Wyatt almost choked on his bacon. Sam slapped him on the back and scowled at her. "Yeah, he's a real fine catch. What do you mean too old? He ain't old."

Amanda got tickled despite her horror at the situation. "I didn't say he was too old. He said I was too young. But he is right, there is too big a difference in our ages."

"Hogwash!" Applegate grunted. "Thar's plenty of folks married with that many of

years between them. It ain't like y'alls in
school anymore. Them years don't matter a
lick after you get past yor teens."

Amanda could only see this conversation
going downhill from here. She dug into her
toast—not that she was the least bit hungry
anymore—and kept her head down. If they
didn't get out of here soon she feared the
fellas would grab the visiting preacher and
have them hitched before the lunch rush
came through the doors.

"Fellas, stop," Wyatt commanded. "Let
Amanda eat her breakfast in peace. My
brother is getting married soon. It's his
wedding y'all need to be concentrating on."

Stanley's hand holding his black checker
hovered in midair. "The ladies have that'un
under control. Seth was in here with Susan
about an hour ago. Them two is so in love they
didn't even *try* to hide thar goo-goo eyes."

"Yup," Applegate barked. "Only thang
holdin' them up is you gettin' well enough to
walk down the aisle."

Wyatt's expression darkened and
Amanda couldn't miss the muscle jerk in
his jaw. "I told them not to wait on me when
I was in the hospital. Now that I'm on this

cane, there's going to be a wedding soon. I can promise you that."

All three men grinned from ear to ear.

Sam filled Wyatt's coffee cup up. "Now that right thar sounds like you, son. That's always been yor strong point, takin' charge and pushin' forward. We was plenty worried when all you wanted ta do was sit in that house out thar and mope."

"Mope. I was doing no such thing."

Applegate grunted and Stanley spit sunflowers.

"Suit yourself." Applegate lined his black checkers up on the board. "But when a man is so knotted up with anger that he don't get out of the house, that thar is moping."

Stanley stood up. "We've got to get over to play practice. Y'all should come out to the theater sometime. We do the lights and the sound. It would be a good date fer y'all."

"We might do that." Wyatt took a swig of coffee and met her gaze over the rim of his cup. She'd pretty much decided to keep her mouth shut on this entire conversation. Beside that, she was interested in what they were revealing about Wyatt despite the talk about them…but she even found that fascinating—not that she'd let them know it. No, she'd realized that there were some things you kept to yourself in Mule Hollow.

A little while later, they eased out of the diner to the booming encouragement for Wyatt to take Amanda out on a real date. Wyatt didn't say anything until they were in the SUV.

"Well, that didn't exactly go the way I'd planned."

Amanda laughed so hard her shoulders shook as she drove the vehicle toward home. "It was totally unexpected for me, too." Boy, was that the understatement of the year. She'd relaxed some during all of the conversation, though, and that was a good thing. Now, however, alone with him again, she started tensing up.

He adjusted his arm, looking for a more comfortable position, and he watched her as he did it. She didn't look at him but knew he was because she could feel his gaze on her.

"At the meeting with the ladies I went to with Melody the other day, it seemed like the wedding plans were set."

"Yes. Seth told me that Chance has that weekend off, so he'll be coming to do the service. With the PBR it runs a pretty hectic schedule, so it's a good time."

Amanda knew that PBR stood for Pro Bull Riding organization and had been fascinated at the planning meeting when she'd learned that Chance was a preacher. He was Wyatt's cousin on his dad's side and had been raised up with them half their life, whenever his dad hadn't been able to take him on the rodeo circuit during the school year. "That's something I never thought about as a career, but it is wonderful." She really thought so. What a great witness.

"Chance is a great guy. He has a heart of gold and a mission to preach God's word to those bull riders."

Amanda liked that. She'd been sharing her witness with the kids when she worked with them. She wasn't sure what she was doing now. Running?

"I need to check on Melody's garden. Would you like to ride over there with me?" She was asking for trouble by spending more time with Wyatt, but she suddenly didn't want to go back to that tiny trailer at the stagecoach house.

"Sure. Maybe you'll finally tell me why you don't want to talk about your jogging?"

And there it was. Right back to square one. "It's no big deal. I like to run, okay. I just didn't tell you."

"But why? We both know your running is a big deal. I looked it up. A runner with a leg missing above the knee has a much harder time running with a prosthetic. You make it look easy. You run like a deer."

Not only had he been watching her every morning, he'd done research on her condition. Amanda's heart fluttered at the thought. She pulled to a stop beside the green garden. It was surrounded by a tall fence, which Melody had told her was to keep the deer out. The old fence had been described as having some of the original wood from the stagecoach house. Amanda liked the look of the garden, but it wasn't the garden she was thinking about as she climbed from the SUV.

"Yes, I was fourteen at the time of the accident. And all I wanted to do was keep running." She stared across the hood at Wyatt. The man was persistent. And the sun gleaming off his dark hair made him look all too dashing—she'd never in her life used that word before, but it just fit. She could imagine him dressed in his tuxedo for a big benefit ball. He would fit perfectly into that scenario. The wealthy rancher/lawyer—that was the image of him she needed to focus on. That was the life she could never fit into.

And she also couldn't stop thinking about him as a child sitting on the bar stool at Sam's… Wyatt's son would do that one day—that is, when Wyatt brought him to the ranch on weekend visits.

"My parents said I loved to run from the moment I started walking. I decided I wanted to do marathons. So that was why I was on the side of the road the day that man drove over me."

"That's tough to hear every time you say it. It must be even harder to have to repeat to nosey people like me."

It touched her that he would care. "I'm dealing with it. Be careful here," she said, hoping to divert the conversation, but also concerned that Wyatt might hurt himself. "Concentrate on your balance. Use your stomach muscles to stabilize your back."

He was standing close to her, looking down at her with serious eyes. She suddenly felt panic rising, but she couldn't move. She had that overwhelming urge to take a step and wrap her arms around him. To feel the solid strength of his arms about her.

Wyatt shifted to lean against the gate post, and before she realized what he was doing he'd set his cane aside and lifted his hand to her cheek. The feel of his touch should have made her run all the way home, but she couldn't move. She couldn't breathe. She could only think about his touch and the gentle look that came into his eyes as he stared down at her.

"Amanda, I wish you would tell me what is really bothering you. My gut tells me there's more to you giving up working with kids and coming all the way out here. What are you running from?"

Chapter Fourteen

What was he doing? He was stepping over a boundary he hadn't wanted to cross. But Amanda brought something out in him he wasn't used to feeling. He'd been unable to stop himself from touching her. Her deer-in-the-headlights look the instant his fingertips touched her was expected, but he didn't like it. He'd told himself not to do it. But he hadn't been able to stop himself. It had taken everything in him not to demand she tell him earlier. All morning he'd been building up to finding out what was bothering her…or what she was hiding—if she was. "I have to tell you that I think you are an amazing woman."

She shook her head and her eyes slid away from his. Did she not see that? Was that why she downplayed the fact that she was a runner? He had the sudden need to pull her into his arms.

He tucked his fingers into his pockets instead and forced them to stay there.

"Come on, Amanda, I know we've had our issues, but I really am a good listener. If you need a friend right now I'm here. Did this guy hurt you? Do something you haven't said?" She wanted to tell him, he sensed that she did with every fiber of his being. *Come on, Amanda. Talk to me.*

"Why are you so certain?"

She was still fighting it. "Because too much points to something being wrong. You love kids and yet you've given that up. Yes, you've been through a hard breakup, but most people would find comfort in doing what they love. You said you loved working with kids…so why aren't you? And why do your beautiful eyes get the saddest expression at times? I saw it at church the other day."

She looked shocked, and he wasn't sure if it was because he'd noticed so much about her or because he'd called her eyes beautiful. But as quick as she looked shocked, the sadness flooded her eyes.

He couldn't help himself. "What is it, Amanda?" He reached for her. To his surprise, she came into his arms and buried her head against his shoulders. Her tremble vibrated through him and he tightened his arms about her. Feelings of protectiveness like nothing he'd ever felt before surged over him. Amanda was right up there as being one of the bravest—if not *the* bravest—people he'd ever known. So what had her so shaken?

"I'm sorry," she mumbled against his shoulder. She was so tense that he began rubbing the muscles between her shoulder blades in a gentle circular motion.

"Talk to me." He was treading on quicksand. Amanda was in his arms, and he was going to have a hard time letting her go when she decided to back away from him.

But she didn't move away. She took a deep breath and looked up at him.

She glanced out past the tomato bushes before pinning him with surprisingly clear eyes. Too clear, maybe.

"When Jonathan broke up with me, it was because—" Amanda shook her head. "I can't…I can't talk about it."

Wyatt tried to follow what she was trying to tell him. She'd said she couldn't blame Jonathan for calling off the engagement. That he'd made the right decision for both of them. That it was better to know it up front than later on. Wyatt agreed on all counts. She *was* better off without the guy. Still, he found no place in his heart for understanding the man. You did not tell a woman you loved her and then call it off. When a real man said those words, he meant them. There was no turning back. Wyatt had never found anyone who'd ever tempted him to even think about it.

But he'd never met anyone like Amanda. The thought should have thrown him, but it didn't. Amanda was a woman well worth loving. Did she not feel like she was? Was that the problem?

"You're hurting," Amanda said. "What am I thinking? I've had you trapped here. Let's get you back to the house."

"I'd rather you talk to me." She was closing him out.

"There are just some things I can't put words to, Wyatt."

"Try. It might help."

Instead of answering him she walked away. His hip and back strained as he pushed himself to cross the ground to catch her. "Amanda, I know you and I got off on the wrong foot. I was an idiot, but I hope you consider me a friend."

She turned back to him, her beautiful aquamarine eyes glistening with unshed tears. "Thank you, Wyatt. I like the idea of you being my friend. But—"

Wyatt's heart clutched, and he wanted to pull her back into his arms and comfort her. "You are a remarkable woman, Amanda. I hope you know that."

"I can't do this, Wyatt. What I'm dealing with is something I have to deal with on my own."

She walked around to the truck and got in. Her statement only caused more questions. He should back off. Give her what she wanted.

It was none of his business.

But, staring at her through the windshield, he knew he wasn't going to be able to do that.

Amanda couldn't forget the feel of being in Wyatt's arms a few minutes earlier in the

garden. Or that she'd almost told him everything! It had been only by sheer willpower
that she'd stopped herself before revealing
how totally empty she felt inside. Knowing
Wyatt, he wouldn't have understood that at
all.

He'd have tried to comfort her. As he'd
done so sweetly before. She'd been grateful
for his concern, but she didn't want his
sympathy.

As it was, she was having a hard time
figuring out how to handle this new relationship they'd begun. He'd wanted to be her
friend. And he'd said such nice things about
her—she felt awkward believing that he
thought she was remarkable. And yet he'd said
so.

As she waited for him to stretch out on the
table, she tried not to think about how nice
it had felt to be in his arms. It had been just
as comforting as she'd suspected it would
be…even if she'd thrown herself at him. But
it had been so much more.

Unbidden, she suddenly wondered how
there couldn't be a woman in Wyatt's life.
Melody and his brothers had said no, but
maybe there was someone they didn't know

about. He could have a whole little black book or he could as easily be free and unencumbered.

Just like she was—free as a bird to date whomever she wanted.

That thought had her staring down at her bare ring finger. When she'd talked to Wyatt earlier, she'd realized that she had absolutely no feelings for Jonathan. Hadn't for a while.

There was no lingering sadness at the idea of Jonathan's ring not being there. The only sadness—the deep, neverending sadness—was the reason his ring wasn't on her finger.

I want children of my own. His words seeped through her soul like unshed tears filling her up on the inside.

She'd told herself there was no reason to dwell on it. God had a plan for her life and it wasn't to have children. She would find a way to come to terms with that. Just as she'd found a way to come to terms with the fact that she had only one leg.

Someday she'd understand what His plan was where children were concerned. She just had to deal with the ups and downs she faced until that time came. And right now she had to figure out what to talk to Wyatt about.

"Do you compete in marathons?"

His question was like a gift, as if he knew she needed help. "I do two or three a year, but nothing major. My priority has been my work. After I realized that it gave me a purpose when I lost my leg, I backed off from the running."

"But the running is also a way to reach and inspire people." He glanced over his shoulder at her.

"Oh, I believe so, too. It's just that I was so busy with my work with the kids that I didn't have the time to train as heavily as I needed to. I enjoyed helping kids gain confidence after losing their limbs. There is nothing like watching a kid walk for the first time after…" She faltered, realizing she'd started talking about her work as if it was as natural as breathing. She remembered how rewarding her work had been. Only twenty minutes earlier she'd been in tears thinking about it.

"I can see where that would be rewarding. It's worthwhile. It means something, Amanda."

"I know it does." But that didn't mean she could go back to it.

"Do you think you'll be able to go back to working with kids later on?" he asked gently.

He was reading her mind. "I don't think so," she said.

"Why?" He looked over his shoulder again. His eyes sharp. Digging. "Why is that? I have a feeling you were great with kids. You said you loved it."

"I have my reasons. How does this feel?" She pressed a knot too hard to distract him. He jerked.

"Hurts," he gritted. "If I didn't know better I'd say you did that on purpose."

"Well, I did, but only because I need to in order to make it better. You know that."

She was testy. But this was not what she wanted to talk about. How in the world had she let this conversation go to this?

"Why can't you go back to doing what you love? What is it that you aren't telling me?"

That did it! The man was entirely too inquisitive. Maybe it was because he was a lawyer. "Wyatt, I'm not on the stand. I've made it clear that I don't want to talk about this."

His brows dipped. "When a client goes on the defensive like that it's not a good thing."

Amanda's brows did some major dipping of their own. "See, that's where you are obviously confused. I am not your client. You are mine." With that she turned and marched out the door.

Unprofessional—you bet.

But she didn't care anymore. The man needed to back off. And he needed to do it now.

Chapter Fifteen

"You look beautiful!" Amanda stood inside Ashby's Treasures, the dress store beside Lacy's Heavenly Inspirations. It was a cute boutique store that carried a little bit of everything—even bridal dresses! When Susan had called and asked Amanda to come see her dress, she'd been honored to be included. She'd also been glad to get away for a little while.

The dress was white with beading along the edge of the bodice and along the bottom.

To go with the dress, Lacy had swept Susan's blond hair into a soft style that exposed her neckline. Amanda thought all brides were beautiful, but she didn't think she'd ever seen a happier one.

Amanda hadn't known exactly how she would handle seeing a bride, but she'd felt as if she would be fine. It had been a shock to realize how little it bothered her not to be marrying Jonathan.

She wasn't certain that she'd even loved Jonathan. He had been convenient—was that the right word? It made her sound so horrible. But the truth hurt sometimes, and she was afraid that she'd convinced herself that she was in love with him because he was willing to marry her even though she was damaged. She hated that word, but what else was she? She couldn't have children. That couldn't be fixed. *Damaged* seemed an appropriate word choice. She needed to face reality and move on.

"Susan, I think everything works great together," Lacy said from where she was standing beside the mirror. "Amanda and Ashby, what do y'all think?"

"You're beautiful, Susan," Amanda said. "And I love the hair the way you did it, Lacy."

Ashby was smoothing Susan's train out. "I think it's perfect. This dress was meant for you."

Susan was studying her slim, elegant reflection in the mirror. "I love it. I'm so excited I don't know what to do." She met Amanda's gaze in the mirror. "I can't thank you enough for coming here and helping Wyatt. If it weren't for you he would be miserable and I wouldn't be standing here yet."

"He's doing great. His arm is doing well. I told him yesterday that he could start using it. He tried to hide it but he was really happy about that." She had gotten secretly tickled at the macho way he took the news. He'd clearly wanted to jump up and down and do flips, but instead he'd nodded and just flexed his arm. Of course he'd thanked her—carefully. They were both treading on eggshells around each other. He at least was taking her hint and not asking her personal questions for now, and for that she was thankful.

"So what are you going to do when this job is over?" Susan asked.

"She's going to stay in Mule Hollow," Lacy chimed in.

Ashby smiled. "You can't go wrong moving here. I love it."

"I've thought about it. I really have." That got big smiles from both of them. "From the first moment I drove into town and saw

Adela's Apartments. I've thought about it. But I can't."

"Why not?" Lacy crossed the room to be closer. "You like it here, don't you?"

"Yes, she does," Susan answered for her. "I can tell. And Wyatt would be happy if you did that."

"Wyatt will be in Dallas. Besides, there is nothing going on between us that he would care one way or the other if I stayed or not. Besides, my job would make moving here impossible." That might not have been true, and she knew it.

Susan and Lacy looked at each other and shook their heads as if she was totally missing the big picture. She wasn't—they just didn't have all the facts.

"Wyatt will be back and forth." Susan reached for the hook at the neck of the gown. Amanda moved to help her. "Thank you," she said, then continued talking. "We are hoping someday soon he'll decide to come home for good and help with the ranches. Until then, if you were in town that would give him more reasons for coming home."

Amanda laughed nervously. "Y'all, I'm

his physical therapist. Not his girlfriend. And like I said, my job could make the move impossible."

"You could be. And nothing is impossible," Lacy said, not giving up.

"*Lacy,* I could not be. Besides that, I would never fit into his lifestyle in Dallas. I'm not a black-tie-event type person and he reeks of it. I'm also—"

"That is a no-brainer," Lacy said, rolling her blue eyes. "You can fit in anywhere."

"That's true," Susan added, heading toward the dressing room. Ashby followed and held the dressing room door open for her. Susan paused. "Why would you even think you wouldn't fit in?"

"I don't want to fit in. I'm a simple girl. I like blue jeans and running shoes. I don't like dressing up and mingling."

"So does this mean you aren't coming to my wedding?"

"Of course I'm coming. I wouldn't miss it for the world."

"That's what I hoped you'd say. See you in a minute and then we can all go to lunch."

"Are you all right?" Lacy asked when they were alone.

"Sure. Why?"

Lacy studied her. "Because you look so sad."

"I just had something on my mind, but I'm good."

"Are you sure? I'm a good listener." Her eyes sparkled with compassion.

Amanda shook her head; she just couldn't talk about it. "I'm fine. Really."

"I don't believe you, but I'm not going to press you. If you need to talk, I'm here. Oh, and don't try to get out of coming Friday night to Susan's party at my house, either. I'll come chuck you in my car and haul you there kicking and screaming if I have to."

Amanda laughed. "I'd like a ride in that car." Lacy was the owner of the ancient Cadillac convertible. They matched since they both looked like fun.

Lacy grinned. "Then you'll have one. I love my car. It's different and makes me happy."

"I think it matches you," Amanda said. "You are unique. I love that about you."

"Well, thank you! When my baby is born, the one thing I want him or her to know is that God loves people who aren't afraid to be the way He made them. I love that in my job

I get to witness to people every day. And hopefully make folks smile—even if it is just because I talk too much."

"There is way more to you than that! I like that you are sure of who you are and what you're here to do." Amanda knew Lacy witnessed in everything she did, so that was no surprise. It made Amanda feel like she was failing the Lord even more than she'd already been feeling. She'd walked away from her kids and now, since being here with Wyatt, had she done anything that could possibly be called a witness?

"Don't keep patting me on the back," Lacy said, waving her pink-tipped fingernails. "Believe me, God has His hands full keeping me in line. That's what's so great about Mule Hollow. I just love all the friends I've made since being here. We keep each other straight and help out and pray for each other. We have each other's backs. How about you, Amanda? Does someone have your back?"

Amanda hesitated and Lacy winked at her. "You should really think about staying. I'm serious. Logistically, it might make your job harder—but something could probably be figured out about that. Believe me, though, if you pray about it and God leads you to hang out with us, then you should stay."

Amanda sighed. It was tempting. It really, really was.

"But just so you know, you've been given a reprieve on the matchmaking efforts of Norma, Esther and Adela. They have been so distracted by trying to find preachers to come in on Sunday that they haven't had the time they usually do to try and get something going with you and Wyatt."

"They know I'm leaving and that wouldn't work."

Lacy laughed. "Girlfriend, don't you know that those three don't know anything of the kind? They know God has put you and Wyatt here right now. And they know that you are single and so is he. And they also know that there've been sparks flying between y'all from day one. To them that's like waving a red flag."

Amanda hated that they were having a hard time finding a preacher, but she was glad they had something distracting them. The last thing she needed right now was a posse after her in full pursuit!

* * *

Wyatt had made a huge mistake. He'd pushed Amanda too hard and now she'd withdrawn from him. She did her job, but if he so much as looked like he was going to get personal with her, she clammed up. He'd been praying for guidance and hoped that she might talk with Lacy or Susan. All he knew was she needed to talk to someone.

"So did you have a good time with Susan and Lacy yesterday?" Wyatt asked when she came in the next morning.

"Yes, I did. It was a good trip."

She looked more at ease than she had the last couple of days, and that made him happy. He couldn't stop thinking about her. Couldn't stop wanting to give her a reason to smile. He'd been praying lately—something he'd let slide over time—that God would help her with the struggle she was having. He wished she would feel comfortable enough to confide in him. He'd started to care about Amanda, and he couldn't even pinpoint when it had happened. It had just happened.

When it came to Amanda, his unsureness was a new experience for him. Even different from the lack of confidence he'd felt about his recovery when she'd arrived. For a man who'd had all the confidence in the world just a couple of months earlier, his world had been shaken up on all corners.

"Susan and Cole are going to be happy." *That* he was confident of.

"You made a good match, Mr. Turner."

He was pleased by her teasing tone and the sparkle in her soft eyes. It was starting off like a good day. "I just saw the obvious and acted on it."

She tilted her head to the side. "And what was the obvious?"

"There was just an electricity in the air when they set eyes on each other. And then later at the reception Susan seemed to make something in Cole come alive that I hadn't seen since his fiancée died."

"I didn't know about that." Amanda's heart hurt for Cole.

"He had a hard time. But he went on with his life at the same time. He was even his happy-go-lucky self at times, but it took time. When he saw Susan, I just had a gut feeling that something could come of it."

"Well, I think that's great. Susan was so happy yesterday. She looked beautiful in her dress. Which brings us to your therapy. I want us to head outside today. We need to try different surfaces to build your balance. Are you up for that?"

The phone rang and he started to reach for it but stopped. This was important. And he wanted to continue his conversation with Amanda. Nothing was urgent that was happening in the office. He also knew from the tiny movement of Amanda's jaw and the slight quirk at the edge of her lips that she was fighting patience with him and his work. "I'm up for it," he said, standing up slowly and feeling his hip strain. It was getting better, and walking always seemed to help it. "Is now a good time for you?"

Amanda didn't try to hide her pleasure at him choosing therapy over work. Only she was wrong, it was therapy with *her* he'd just chosen over the call.

Wyatt had a good heart. An unselfish heart that was easy to see and she liked that. Amanda and Wyatt were walking down the gravel road with cattle grazing on either side of them. She was amazed at his perception and intuition in intervening in his brothers' lives in order to help them find the loves of their lives. One day he would find the love of his life and the lucky lady would be getting a jewel. But today, she was walking with him in the pasture.

If she moved to Mule Hollow, would he come home more? Would he come home to see her? Lacy and Susan had her thinking.

Pushing the thought away, she watched him walk. His gait was improving, but there was still a way to go. The hitch in his hip movement remained very pronounced. She'd hoped to have him in better shape for the wedding just because she knew he would like to walk down the aisle as normally as possible. "Your persistence is paying off."

"Thanks to you. Lucky me to have you in my corner."

Amanda's heart skipped a few beats as she met his serious eyes. It would be so easy to let her emotions lead her right now. But emotions were deceiving. She'd learned that with Jonathan. "You would have done great with anyone."

His brows dipped. "I don't think so. You taught me more about courage and real strength than anyone else could have because of what you've been through and how you handled it."

Others she'd seen had been through much more than she had. "There are kids out there who have been through far more than me. Kids who don't have the money to have the best prosthetics or the money to continue therapy that will enable them to walk without limps. But they keep on working at it even after I'm pulled off the job. Those are the ones who have really been through it."

"See, that's what I love about you," Wyatt said. "You will not let anyone feel bad for you. You are determined to keep your chin up and think positive. And to think of others."

That's what I love about you. Amanda's heart had stopped at the words. Oh, she knew it wasn't true. She knew it was just quirky word choice. Still…

She pushed her hair behind her ear and concentrated on the road. There were rough spots along this stretch and while she was watching his gait she could very easily forget to think about her own. "You give me too much credit."

"You give yourself too little."

She smiled at that. "You have an argument for everything."

His lips curved up slowly. "I am what I am."

"That is the understatement of the decade."

"You are as much an avoider of questions as I am at pushing them."

Amanda stopped walking and he did, too. A swallow flew by being chased by another. They dipped and dived—much like the conversation. Wyatt wasn't going to let her get away with forgetting that she hadn't told him everything. And maybe she really didn't want to. "I've realized I didn't love Jonathan," she said unexpectedly.

"Really." His surprise couldn't be disguised, but to his credit his expression remained neutral.

"We should start back before you overdo it and your back starts to tighten up." She began walking slowly back the way they'd come. Wyatt fell into step beside her, his gait slow but steady. She gave him a sideways glance, knowing she had to look as embarrassed as she felt. "I think I let my emotions convince me that I was in love with him. It had taken me so long to decide to go out—I had pretty much convinced myself that no man would ever want me. And here, on my first venture out, I'd found one. It's embarrassing."

Wyatt's hand on her arm stopped her. "Amanda, why would you not think someone would want you? You are a special woman."

His eyes glittered with anger. Amanda went breathless, she was so startled. She hadn't meant to say what she'd said. She'd been talking about her being barren—he wouldn't know that. How careless of her. She'd let her guard down.

"I don't like what I'm hearing. Amanda, any man would be blessed to have you fall in love with him."

What about you? She was treading on dangerous ground—stupid ground was what it was. Looking into his eyes in that moment, she didn't care.

When Wyatt leaned in and kissed her, Amanda's heart stopped.

Wyatt tugged her close. Dropping his cane, he wrapped both arms around her and sent her world spinning out of control as he deepened his kiss.

Amanda knew she was never, ever, ever going to be the same after this moment.

She was falling in love with Wyatt.

I want children of my own. Jonathan's words hit her.

"Stop." Her voice didn't sound like herself as she pushed Wyatt away. "This is a bad idea."

Wyatt let her go and, to her surprise, he looked as dazed as she felt.

"You might be right. I shouldn't have done that."

She reached for his cane, trying not to let his agreement cut her to the core. But it did. Straightening, she handed the cane to him. "We should get back. Your hip is going to need attention after this long walk."

"Amanda. It's nothing personal," he said quietly.

She felt ill. "You're right, Wyatt. This is business. And only business. We should never have crossed the line. Now, let's get back. You have a bachelor party to go to in a couple of hours and your hip needs some rest."

He didn't say anything as they walked back toward the stagecoach house. Amanda had

Chapter Sixteen

❧

"What's going on between you and Amanda?" Cole straightened his tie and turned to Wyatt. "Is this straight?"

Cole, Seth, Wyatt and their cousin Chance were waiting inside the back room of the sanctuary before the wedding started. Wyatt had been asked that same question several times the night before at the bachelor party. Even Chance had asked him what was wrong thirty minutes after he'd arrived yesterday. For a man who'd been known to have inherited his poker face from his great-great-great-great-great-grandpa Oakley—the best poker player in seven counties—Wyatt wasn't holding up so well. Try as he might, he couldn't hide the fact that he'd made a huge error in judgment. The guilt of that error must have been written all over him because it was obvious he wasn't fooling anyone.

"Cole, I told you last night at your party that nothing was wrong. This is your wedding day. You're supposed to be thinking about Susan walking up that aisle, not about your big brother. I'm flattered and all, but come on, bro, give a man a break. Susan wouldn't be too happy if she knew."

"He's right, you know," Seth said, slapping him on the back. "Little brother, this is a great day. Don't think about anything but you and her. I'll get big brother straightened out while you're on your honeymoon."

Cole chuckled. "Thanks. It's the greatest day, but it wouldn't be happening if it weren't for you, Wyatt, so its only fitting that I be thinking about you, too."

Cole's grin was as big as Wyatt had ever seen it.

"All I did was act on a hunch. You did the rest."

Seth thumbed his black hat off his forehead and settled speculative eyes on Chance. "You might want to get Wyatt to act on a hunch for you. After all, you aren't getting any younger, you know," Seth teased.

Dark-headed like the rest of them, Chance had the Turner look of lean jawline and crooked grin, only his eyes weren't shades of blue but as green as clover.

He just shook his head. "I haven't found a woman yet who was willing to put up with my schedule, and I'm not planning to stop my work." They all knew that was how he felt. Chance took his work very seriously. "I love preaching to those cowboys before they ride. I've got Christian cowboys and unbelievers alike coming to services. God's put me where He has and until He tells me different I'll be standing right outside the turnout gate every Sunday when my cowboys ride." He turned serious green eyes on Wyatt. "How about you? When are you going to settle down? I'm prepared to be a bachelor for the rest of my life if that's what God has planned for me."

Wyatt respected Chance and his uncommon faith. Any man who thought God didn't save the roughest of the bunch could just look at his cousin and they would know the redemptive power of God's grace. Chance had dedicated his life to serving the Lord. He did so among the men he'd competed with and counted as friends for years.

As for Wyatt, he hadn't really thought about his marrying status until lately. He'd been so intent on getting his brothers married off so the Turner name could be carried on. And just because he felt responsible for them. He'd known his parents would want them to be happy and he'd been determined to see that done.

Prior to the plane crash he'd been satisfied with his life tenfold. Now, he wasn't sure of anything except that he'd caused Amanda pain.

Yesterday he'd not been able to stop himself from kissing her. She'd made that statement about not thinking a man would want her—how could she think that? It had to have come from the breakup...*and her lack of a leg?* Maybe. The idea stunned him. How had Jonathan been so cruel? How had *he* been so cruel? He'd kissed her before he'd thought things through. He wasn't ready to settle down. His life was in Dallas and Amanda's life was wherever the next job took her. Even if he was ready to settle down, the logistics wouldn't work. He'd cared for her for a while now, and he wanted the best for her. She deserved the best. Not another man messing with her heart.

What was best for her was for him not to think about how she'd felt in his arms. Or how one touch of her lips... Wyatt stopped right there and pushed thoughts of kissing Amanda out of his mind. This was Cole's wedding. He needed to focus on Cole and Susan.

He did not need his brothers and his cousin asking him what was going on in his brain because he was too distracted to keep up with where their conversation had gone while he had Amanda on his mind.

"Okay, it's time, ladies," Norma Sue commanded, entering the dressing room. She and Esther Mae were the wedding planners and were taking their positions seriously. Amanda had shown up early when she'd driven Wyatt to the church, and Melody and Susan had drawn her into the dressing room with them and Lacy. Melody was the maid of honor and Lacy was the bridesmaid. Amanda was hired to help and was having trouble. Had been since the kiss.

"It sure is," Esther Mae said, hustling in behind Norma Sue. She had on a purple dress topped off with a purple-and-white hat with a riot of morning glories encircling the rim. "You should see those men. I tell you, they marched out there in those black, Western suits and those black Stetsons and I thought I was going to pass slap out right there in the doorway."

Norma Sue had traded in her overalls for a pink striped dress without a hat. She ducked her chin and looked down her nose at her friend. "That would have been a catastrophe in more ways than one. We'd a had to just roll you out of the way and gone on with this wedding. After the plane crash we are not letting anything get in the way of marrying off these two."

"Norma Sue," Susan said. "We would not have rolled Esther Mae out of the way."

"Now, Susan," Lacy said, smoothing her pale blue dress down. "We would have had to because if we didn't we wouldn't have been able to get the door open to get you inside."

Esther Mae harrumphed. "I didn't pass out, so hush, Norma Sue, and let's get these gals lined up and ready so Adela can start playing the wedding march."

"Amanda, you got the train?" Norma Sue opened the door.

"Yes, ma'am. I do." Amanda carefully gathered up the short train and smiled at Susan, who suddenly looked nervous.

"I'm so excited I can hardly breathe." She placed a hand on her stomach and took a deep breath, meeting Amanda's gaze with bright eyes.

"Oh, that's a good thing," Esther Mae called, waving them toward the door like she was directing traffic. "Just don't pass out or Norma Sue might send someone up that aisle for you…" She paused her traffic signals and grinned at Amanda. "We could always send Amanda in to marry Wyatt and then when you wake up we could continue with your ceremony."

All attention was suddenly riveted to Amanda. Lacy hooted behind her flower bouquet while everyone else laughed.

Norma Sue hiked a brow. "We could do that even if Susan keeps her wits about her."

"Y'all are crazy." Amanda laughed—it was the only thing to do. They never stopped. She wondered if Wyatt was getting harassment on his end. How embarrassing that would be. "Susan is the only bride in town today, so come on and let's get her in there before the groom passes out."

Or before poor Wyatt's hip and back gave out on him from having to stand for so long. He'd made great progress, but standing in one spot for long periods of time wasn't good for him.

As they all finally exited the annex building and started down the sidewalk, Amanda felt a surge of anticipation that rippled through her and settled in the pit of her stomach. Wyatt had looked fantastic in his suit. As they stepped up onto the church's porch, Amanda's knees felt weak thinking about him. Would she ever have a wedding?

"Amanda," Esther Mae said, "spread that out here and then you come stand by the door with me and Norma Sue while the vows are exchanged."

Lacy looked over her shoulder at her and winked. "Yeah, that way when Susan and Cole both pass out they can send you right on in as the pinch hitter."

Amanda laughed again. But the next second Norma Sue tapped lightly on the door and Applegate stuck his head in and gave a frown.

"It's about time," he snapped. His voice cracked like a cannon over the soft music Adela was playing and the entire church of folks turned to look at them. "We about figured we had a runaway bride on the loose."

Chuckles erupted through the sanctuary.

"Not hardly," Norma Sue grunted. "I'd tell you to give the signal so we can get these two lovebirds married off finally, but you done alerted the whole place, so move out of the way. We're coming through."

Adela switched music and Norma Sue practically shoved Lacy over the threshold. The wedding was on.

But from the back of the bride Amanda had had eyes for only one person the moment Applegate had swung the doors open. Wyatt, broad-shouldered and taller by an inch than the others, locked his gaze on to her, too. For the life of her, Amanda couldn't look away.

Norma Sue patted Amanda's hands, reminding her to let go of the train, as she leaned in close. "Uh-huh. That man can't take his eyes off of you."

"I think it's romantic," Esther Mae hissed

in her other ear as the three of them scooted over to stand at the back of the church so they could see over everyone's heads.

Amanda looked from one beaming grin to the other as Adela ended the wedding march and everyone sat down. She felt the posse suddenly closing in on her as Esther Mae nudged her and Norma Sue leaned in again.

"That's a good man right yonder."

Amanda could have kissed Wyatt right then and there because he wasn't looking at her. His attention was focused on Cole and Susan as they took hands—just as it should be.

If he'd have been looking at her again she wouldn't have had any kind of chance to stop the matchmaking plans spinning around in the posse's heads.

Thankfully, his attention was exactly where it should have been. It was her *own* that was misbehaving.

Wyatt knew. He listened to the vows that Chance spoke to Susan and Cole and his gaze kept locking on Amanda. She was standing in between Norma Sue and Esther Mae, and he caught her looking to him as frequently.

"To have and to hold from this day forward." When Chance spoke those vows, Wyatt knew Amanda was the woman he wanted to marry. How he knew it—when he hadn't even realized he loved her—was a mystery to him. But just as he'd known when he met Melody and then Susan that they were the women for his brothers, he knew it with everything in him that Amanda Hathaway was the woman for him.

He'd never felt the protectiveness that he felt with her. She was somewhat lost right now, and though he'd been deeply troubled when she'd come along, she'd helped him. She'd put away her own problems and pulled him back from the dark emotions he'd been trapped in. He hadn't thought of his own problem since the morning he'd seen her running. The morning after she'd stood up to him and pointed out what blessings God had bestowed on him. The morning after she'd said all that and not pointed out anything about her own lost leg or the things she'd had to suffer through. She'd told him what he needed to hear and she'd done it without any self-pity whatsoever. He loved and admired that.

He loved what she stood for. He loved how

she stood her ground with him. But most of all he loved her spirit. She'd chosen to look at what God had in store for her and to move forward with a purpose.

And now, though he knew something was eating at her, he loved the way she was fighting it…and he knew she was. She would have confided in him, or someone else, if it weren't true.

She was alone and he wanted her to know he was there for her…wanted her to know that she could lean on him.

For the rest of their lives.

He hadn't given marriage a thought before now, but he knew he was going to marry Amanda.

The wedding was beautiful. Chance gave a traditional ceremony, which was Amanda's favorite ceremony and what she'd wanted for her own wedding.

Wyatt was in great spirits as they drove to the wedding reception. He seemed more at ease and relaxed than he ever had, and she attributed it to the fact that he'd accomplished what he'd set out to do when he'd decided it was time to marry off his brothers.

Again she was struck by what a romantic he was. Home and hearth meant everything to him.

She'd struggled the entire service not to stare, but she'd known he was watching her. Even with Esther Mae and Norma Sue flanking her, he'd repeatedly found her gaze across the sanctuary. And each time her heart squeezed and her stomach filled with butterflies. Oh, how she wished…

She couldn't let herself finish that wistful thought. Life and love with Wyatt was not a possibility.

"You did a good thing," she said as she parked in front of the community center.

He surprised her by reaching for her hand. "Are you all right?"

Her skin burned where he touched her and she wanted to pull away but couldn't. "Yes, I'm fine."

"I hope so. The ceremony didn't bring back bad memories or hurtful ones?" His thumb was making gentle circles on the back of her hand.

"No." She could hardly speak. All she could think about was the feel of his hand on hers. The tender way he was looking at her and the overwhelming need to be in his arms. Being with Wyatt had helped her in so many ways. "I actually thanked God for not letting the marriage with Jonathan go through. I didn't love him and I know that completely and clearly now."

Wyatt's eyes darkened. "I'm glad. You deserve a man who is going to love you with all his heart and give you all the good things you deserve."

Amanda's heart dropped. He was squeezing her hand ever so gently, his voice carrying on its husky tone something that confused her. "I'm not going to ever marry." She hadn't meant to say that.

People walked by, laughing and talking as they headed into the reception. But neither of them made a move for the door.

"Why do you say that?"

"Because I have my reasons, Wyatt."

"And what are those reasons? And don't say you can't tell me, Amanda. You need to tell someone what it is that you are dealing with alone. Don't you know I care for you and that with all that you've done for me, I wouldn't do anything to harm you? God put you in my life to change me. And He has. In more ways than you know right now. But I believe He put me in your life to help you. Please talk to me. It's time!"

"We need to go to the reception."

He shook his head. "We need to get to the bottom of this."

"Wyatt, why does it matter to you?"

"Because I care, Amanda—you'd be surprised how much."

Amanda's heart began pounding at his words. "Wyatt—" she said, but lost all train of thought when he touched her cheek.

"Trust me, Amanda. I'm here for you."

"I have nothing to offer y—a man." The words came out before she could stop them. Wyatt's eyes sharpened and his hand stilled. She looked down, her gaze falling on the hand he still held. She loved Wyatt. She knew it, knew it wasn't anything like what she'd thought she felt for Jonathan. She knew she loved this tender man and that there was absolutely nothing she could do about it.

"You said that before. What makes you say that? You have everything to offer."

She took a deep breath; her insides were churning. "I lost more than my leg when I was hit…I lost my ability to have children."

Her words knocked the breath out of him.

"What? Why didn't you tell me?"

"Hey, you two," Seth called from the door. "Cole wants y'all in the picture with them cutting the cake, pronto."

Wyatt scowled.

Amanda grabbed the door handle with shaking hands. "We need to go inside so you can be in the pictures with Cole and Susan," she said, pushing her car door open. "Your family is waiting."

"I want to talk about this," Wyatt growled, grabbing her arm.

"No, Wyatt. This isn't fair. Cole and Susan have waited for you long enough and you know you wouldn't miss this for the world."

He let out an exasperated breath. "You're right. But this is important, Amanda, and we will talk. You can bet on that."

Amanda got out of the car, closed her eyes, praying for help... It seemed hopeless, though.

Chapter Seventeen

He was tired of smiling. Wyatt had smiled for the camera over and over again so that when Cole and Susan looked back over their wedding pictures he wouldn't look angry. He'd already caused them to wait this long to get married, he didn't want to be responsible for ruining their wedding pictures for all of eternity.

But the conversation with Amanda kept playing over and over in his mind. She couldn't have children. She loved children. The thought of it broke his heart.

He couldn't imagine all that Amanda had lived through. Why had she been able to work with kids for so long and now she didn't want to? Couldn't.

Moving to the corner of the room, he leaned against the wall and watched her serving cake with Adela. The reception was a success. Cole and Susan were happy and everyone was having a blast. Norma Sue and Esther Mae worked beside Amanda and Adela serving cake and punch as though it was a free-for-all. It even seemed that Amanda was having a great time as she placed sliced cake onto plates. She smiled at everyone and even laughed when cowboy after cowboy made some comment—flirting with her, no doubt. It hadn't escaped his notice that she had an ever-growing army of admirers. He wondered if any of them could see past her smile to the heartache she was hiding.

One thing about Amanda, she seemed to be able to shut her own needs away and focus on the needs of those around her. Watching her, he wasn't sure if that was a good thing or not.

He wanted to storm across the room, take her in his arms and tell her that he loved her. That it didn't matter if she couldn't have children—was this the reason Jonathan had broken off their engagement? *Had he known when he asked her and then changed his mind?*

The questions wrestled for answers—answers Wyatt would uncover as soon as he and Amanda were alone.

It was late when they finally headed home. The sun was low in the sky and the roads to the stagecoach house glistened white as Amanda followed them toward home. Home. She'd begun to think of this as home in the short few weeks that she'd been here. She knew it was because of Wyatt. She loved him and couldn't imagine leaving here. But she would.

She'd made so many friends, even tonight she'd made more. For a town that only a few years ago had been dying, it was full of life now. Bustling with life. She felt good just having been in the middle of such a positive atmosphere tonight, even after practically breaking down in the car with Wyatt.

Working with Adela had been part of that. "I loved working with Adela tonight," she said, needing something to fill the silence as she drove. "She is a delight."

Wyatt had watched her all night. She knew

that their conversation was inevitable. She'd expected him to practically interrogate her the minute the SUV's doors were closed. But he'd been quiet, lost in thought. It was plain to see, by the distracted look she'd come to recognize in his eyes, that his mind was working overtime. Dread filled her. She'd wanted to tell him for so long about not being able to have children and now...now she'd told him. What was he thinking?

"I'm so sorry, Amanda. Talk to me. Tell me what happened."

His words were a low rumble in the darkness. They reached out to her, urging her to open up.

Amanda took a shallow breath, feeling as if she were treading on quicksand. It was time. "It just recently hit me what I've lost...."

Wyatt stilled his heart as her words flowed, as rough as the cattle guard she drove the SUV over. He was glad they were home. This hadn't been a conversation to have while driving. He'd meant to wait.

She pulled to a stop in front of the house and cut the engine. He waited for her to continue.

"I've dedicated my life to helping kids.

Felt like it was my calling. My purpose. Over the years I came to realize that at fourteen I didn't understand how the complete hyster-ectomy would affect me." Her words were stronger than he'd thought they would be. "I didn't realize how I would one day long…" her voice cracked "…for a baby."

Wyatt could see where at fourteen the loss of her leg would have been the focus of her young life. A kid wouldn't understand that she might one day long for a baby. A kid might only think about having to face life without the leg she'd had before she'd gone into surgery. A woman of twenty-four who saw other women all around her who were expecting children would understand only too well what she'd lost…especially one whose fiancé had broken off their engage-ment. He had to ask. "Did you start strug-gling with this prior to Jonathan breaking the engagement?"

She nodded. "Some. I'd been thinking about it since I was about twenty. But I'd been counting my blessings. Focusing on them and letting God get me through it. But it was getting worse each year. And then, well, I realized the truth."

"And what is that?"

She bit her lip, crossed her arms as if to protect herself. "I'm a woman with one leg and no ability to give a man children. I'm not the prize—" She halted as if unable to continue.

She didn't need to finish her statement. Her view of what that truth was showed in her expression.

"You know that's not right," he said softly, touching her cheek.

"What man would want me under those conditions? I'm not one to beat around the bush or want sympathy. This is fact. I didn't date because of that."

This was something new. "You didn't date?"

She shook her head. "I couldn't handle thinking about someone confirming what I had realized."

Then she'd decided to date Jonathan the jerk. Wyatt shifted in his seat to face her more fully. Amanda needed to talk about this and maybe she needed him to ask frank questions. "What made you change your mind and start dating Jonathan?"

"It just happened. He…" She sighed. "He

was nice and he was persistent. I told him on our second date and he was okay with it."

"But he wasn't."

She looked down at her hands folded tightly in her lap. "No. He wasn't."

Wyatt would have decked the guy if he'd been standing there. How could the man do that? "You are better off without him." She looked pained as she closed her eyes, shaking her head. Wyatt's heart clenched. "Do you still *love* him?" Surely not. She'd said once she was over him, but was she? "You are better off without him."

"No. I don't love him. I can just understand—"

"Stop defending him, Amanda. The man saw a pretty, sweet woman and chased her down. As far as I'm concerned he was looking out for only himself the whole time. He told you what you wanted to hear at the time because it suited him." Anger boiled inside of Wyatt. He sucked in a hard breath and counted to ten as he slowly exhaled. He didn't need to upset Amanda any more. The look on her face told him it was too late. "Is this why you don't work with kids?"

Her eyes darkened with sadness and she nodded.

"Amanda, you can't have children, but you have so much to offer a baby. And all those kids whose lives you've touched. Anyone can look at you and how you've lived your life and know that God is using you. Your life is a testimony. It has been to me. And there is no telling how many others—kids and adults alike—who you've inspired firsthand. God has a plan for you. He wants to prosper you and not to harm you." Wyatt couldn't remember the last time he'd quoted scripture but it felt right to do it now.

Tears formed in her beautiful aquamarine eyes. "They have touched my life…but, Wyatt, I can't do it anymore."

He didn't understand. "Why?"

"When I'm around kids now—" She brushed a tear away and it was all he could do not to reach for her. "It started with Jonathan. It hit me then with full force how big the hole inside me is." She paused, closing her eyes briefly. "I'm dealing with it in my way—here."

"Amanda, there are babies who need adopting. You can do that."

"It's not that…" She faltered as if she almost couldn't get the words out. "It's in here." She flattened her hand to the center of her chest. "I feel so empty. So broken—like I have a hole inside me that can't be filled. Nothing makes it better. No scripture. No prayer. It's just there. And I feel—" she sighed "—worthless."

"Amanda, no—"

She kept on going. "I can't look at kids now without aching so badly inside that I feel as if I'll be sick. It's a horrible thing. It's something I have to deal with." She shifted her shoulders back and lifted her chin. "And I will." She reached for the door handle. "I'm tired, Wyatt. I think I'll head in. Are you okay? Do you need me to help you get inside?"

She was almost bubbly again—clearly a veil over her pain. Wyatt shook his head. "I'm good, Amanda. You go on in and get some sleep. It'll make you feel better."

She didn't look at him as she climbed from the SUV and headed across the yard. She worried him. There was so much he wanted to say and so much he didn't know *how* to say. It felt strange to be in a situation where he didn't have the words. *I love you* were the words that came raging to the forefront of his heart and soul…but was that what she needed to hear right now? She'd heard those words once and they'd been taken back. They'd led or added to the feelings of unworthiness she said she was feeling.

Worthless! She was a jewel.

He just had to find a way to show her.

After Amanda disappeared around the edge of the house, Wyatt got out of the SUV and slammed the door. He winced from the pain that shot through his shoulder. He'd come a long way, but there was still a long haul ahead. Right now the pain didn't compare to what he was feeling for Amanda. Or what she was feeling herself.

She'd come here to help him heal when she had far deeper hidden scars than anyone could know and certainly see.

Grief was a complex emotion. He and his brothers had lived it when their parents had died tragically. It was a death of flesh and blood. A tangible loss that everyone in the community saw and felt. Amanda's grief was different. It was almost intangible—who would know if she didn't tell? Who would comfort her if she didn't expose it? And if she didn't tell anyone, she suffered alone.

Did she not know how precious she was?

This wasn't what he'd expected. She was a fighter, and so he wouldn't have thought that this could kick the wind out of her the way it had. He'd almost told her he loved her but held back. His gut told him now wasn't the time. He'd been messing up ever since Amanda walked into his life. The last thing he wanted to do was speak too soon. He had to help her first…and then pray she felt the same way about him. He had to have a plan before he did anything stupid. But what?

He needed to ride.

Needed to move.

Restless winds rolled across the pasture as unease and uncertainty clashed inside of him. *What did he need to do for Amanda?*

The sun was settling over the trees. Cole and Susan had planned the afternoon wedding and reception so they could make the long drive to the airport in Ranger. Wyatt glanced into the SUV and saw the key still in the ignition. Walking around to the driver's side, he pulled open the door and slid carefully into the seat.

He needed time to think. He needed to ride. Needed the calm he felt when he was around his horses—

Five minutes later, he pulled into the yard of the main house where Seth and Melody lived. He knew they were probably still in town cleaning up after the reception. Driving to the barn, he eased on the brake and got out of the vehicle. His hip and back tightened up but didn't spasm. His shoulder hadn't complained too much, either. It didn't matter as he made his way into the barn.

Why had God not helped Amanda? She'd said nothing had helped her. No scripture. No prayer. Why had God not given her something to ease her pain?

He stopped in front of the black gelding. "Hello, Soot," Wyatt said, rubbing the horse's neck. "How about a ride?"

"Do you think that's a good idea?"

The question startled Wyatt and he looked over his shoulder. Chance was standing in the doorway.

"I don't really care at the moment. What are you doing here? I figured you'd still be in town."

His cousin shrugged and strode over to

prop a boot on the bottom rung of the stall. He patted Soot's neck. "When you were troubled about something, riding always did help you think, didn't it?"

"Same as you."

Chance gave him a Turner grin. "Yup. There's peace out there on those plains."

"I'd almost forgotten how much."

"Do you need to talk?" Chance turned his head and stared at him from beneath the brim of his hat. His serious green eyes bored all the way through Wyatt.

"Nope. I'm fine." It wasn't true and he knew it. But this was a private matter.

"Give me a break. You looked like a cowboy about to get on the rankest bull of the draw and you aren't prepared."

"That bad, huh?"

"Worse. I saw the way you couldn't take your eyes off Amanda all evening. What's going on?"

Maybe counsel from a man of God might help him help Amanda. Wyatt gave in. "This is just between you and me," he clarified.

"This is between you, me and *God*."

Wyatt proceeded to tell him about Amanda's problem. About how she couldn't have children and how she was in a crisis with it now. "She's run here to Mule Hollow trying to find some peace and answers, I think. She's just treading water, hoping God will take away the pain and grief she's feeling, but she's hurting, Chance. And tonight she told me how empty and worthless she feels. That's not good. I don't know what to do for her. She's a remarkable woman. I've never known someone with the heart that she has. She's spent her life inspiring people with the way she's handled losing her leg. She let God take that bad situation and make it good. But this is really hurting her. How can I help her? She is not worthless because she can't bear children."

Chance had been watching him closely. "Man, that's a tough one. First, you can start by doing what you are doing…loving her."

"Is it that obvious?"

Chance placed a hand on his shoulder. "I see it. But I also hear it and see evidence in the concern you're showing her. God puts people into our lives when we need them. It seems to me He's placed you and Amanda in each other's paths at this specific time because it's the right time. Be patient and be there for her like she's been there for you. You're almost back to being yourself because of her care. You can do the same for her. Help her know that this emptiness she's feeling can be filled with God's grace if she'd let it. He's the ultimate comforter and loves her. He'll use this for good, too, if she can let Him. You need to pray about it and then follow God's lead. God doesn't steer us wrong if we can hear His voice when He speaks."

Wyatt stared out into the near darkness, his heart heavy. "But what if I don't feel like I'm hearing God these days?"

"Then wait. Pray and study God's word while you wait, and be patient with yourself. You'll grow during that time. Meanwhile, Amanda needs to know that she isn't less of a woman and that God has made her the way she is for a reason. His love for her is abundant, and though her fiancé forsook her, God never will. *Sometimes* He's quiet because it draws us to seek Him more. He hasn't forsaken you, either, Wyatt. In trials and tribulations God pulls us back to Him. He wants us to rely on Him and not our-selves."

Wyatt closed his eyes and thought about

that. It was so simple. So obvious. "That's me." Unable to be still, he walked toward the outside.

Chance fell into step beside him. "It's all of us sometime or other."

"Yeah, but I've been doing it for so long I didn't see anything wrong with it. I'd begun to think I was invincible. That all I've accomplished was by my own merit and not God's." That was what had been eating at him with crashing the plane. "How can I fix that?" He stopped outside.

Chance smiled easily. "Simple, Wyatt. You've acknowledged it, now just ask God to forgive you and start fresh. The Bible says that when we confess our sins, God forgets it as far as the east is from the west. You believe that, don't you?"

He nodded. "What if I'm not the one to help her? Maybe she should talk to you. You're the preacher."

"He sent you. You're the right man for the job. Go back and talk to her. God will lead you." Chance laid his hand on Wyatt's shoulder. "I'll pray for you both."

"Thanks. I'll need it."

With that said, Chance walked back

toward the house, pure cowboy swagger. If God put people into our lives when we needed them, Wyatt knew there was no mistake in the timing of Chance showing up in the barn. Amanda would be glad to know God had kept him off the horse, he thought as he climbed back into her SUV.

He paused at the cattle guard and stared at the sunset's lingering glow, bowed his head and asked God to forgive him. He prayed God would show him the way to help Amanda…and also the way to win her heart.

Chapter Eighteen

Amanda was waiting on the front porch when she saw headlights winding toward her across the dark pasture. She'd started feeling guilty for not having made certain that Wyatt had gotten inside safely. Yes, he was getting around better and better, but still, he was her patient and she should have walked him to his door. Instead she'd let her emotions—her personal life—interfere with her work.

The last thing she'd expected to find when she'd come to check on him was that her SUV would be gone.

What was he thinking? She headed toward him the minute he pulled to a stop. She had every intention of setting him straight on the issue of driving, but the minute he closed the door she could see something was wrong. He looked nervous in the moonlight.

It was a look she'd never seen on him before.

"Wyatt, is something wrong?" She stopped at the edge of the stagecoach house. He walked steadily toward her and stopped only inches from her. Amanda automatically reached out and touched his arm. As if her touch would calm him. The last thing she needed to do was reach out to Wyatt. But it was becoming an impossibility. He knew everything about her. Her darkest fears and her deepest sorrows. They were connected, and despite everything she'd told him, she'd realized when she'd walked away from him that talking to him had helped her. "Why did you take the car? You aren't ready to drive."

"It doesn't matter. I needed to think. I'm not sure how to approach this, but I can't let you go to sleep tonight without telling you how beautiful you are inside and out." His eyes burned fierce in the starlight. "God did not make a mistake when He made you, or when He allowed everything in your life to happen to you. I've prayed all the way back from the barn for God to lead me on this. I've told myself now isn't the time, but here it is, Amanda."

Holding her captive with his gaze, he stepped up and took her face between his hands. Their warmth seeped into her. "I love you. I love you just the way you are and can only pray that you might someday fall in love with me and let me show you how wonderful you are."

Amanda had gone still when he'd touched her and now on the "I love you" part, joy filled her... Her heart lifted in her chest with a lightness she had never felt. But then reality hit her like an arrow to a balloon.

"No." She took a step back.

"Yes." Wyatt held on, stepping with her. "I'm just giving you warning that I do love you. It may scare you. It may terrify you, and after all you've been through, you have every right to feel that way. But, Amanda Hathaway, I'm a very patient man when I need to be. And I'm very determined, as you well know. So hold on to your hat because I want you for keeps. And I'm going to actively seek to win your heart from this moment forward."

Amanda didn't know what to say. "I'm not going there, Wyatt. I can't—"

"What, risking your heart on someone who truly does love you? Here in Mule Hollow we call that chicken. And there is nothing about you that is chicken."

"Wyatt—" She broke from his tender hands, backing away, only to back straight into the logs of the stagecoach house. Trapped, she was forced to look into his eyes, her heart breaking. "I have nothing to offer you. *Nothing*. Don't you get that?" She looked down at the ground. Didn't he see the truth?

Wyatt took her face in between his hands once more and tilted her head. He stared deeply into her eyes. "I've realized ever so slowly, getting to know you, and as I fell for you, that you hold the key to every dream and aspiration I will ever have. God didn't put us into each other's lives for no reason, Amanda. You are all that I could ever want, and I thank God for sending you into my life when He did."

Amanda felt tears rising as her heart swelled. Her spirit felt buffeted by strong winds, one moment elation, the next desolation. She wanted to run and she wanted to cling to Wyatt and ask him to repeat everything he'd just said. Her locked knees let her do neither one.

Then without warning, Wyatt lowered his head to hers and kissed her. Long and slow. Her insides burned with longing of hopes and dreams long lost.

"I want to marry you," he whispered against her lips.

She gasped. "Don't—"

He pulled back; his arms that had wrapped around her and drawn her into the shelter of his body held her tightly against him. His heart pounded against hers…and she wondered if he could hear the thunder of her blood.

"I love you, Amanda. And I wasn't lying when I said I'm patient. I'm just letting you know this is where I stand and I'm praying you fall in love with me."

She swallowed the words she so wanted to say to him. *I love you, too.* "It would never work."

"Why?"

"Because I can't give you children. You need a little boy who looks like you to sit at Sam's beside you on the bar stool ordering the best food in the world."

"I can have a son with you who can do that if he wants to."

"No—"

"Yes. Amanda, you are a whole and complete woman. God is in you and that makes you whole. The emptiness you feel can be filled with the grace and peace of God if you'll just let it. I did that tonight. I let go of all the anger I'd been feeling—most of it you'd already helped me let go of by just being here and working with me and inspiring me. But I let it go and am going to rethink my life goals. I'm just trying to get you to see that you have to do the same. Face that you are who you are and you are beautiful in every way. Nothing about you is lacking in my eyes or God's. A child out there somewhere desperately needs you to love him or her, or for that matter, a houseful of them. And in my mind I'm the man who God wants to stand there beside you loving them. Please tell me there is a possibility that you could love me back."

Amanda couldn't speak. He had just offered her the world. God was offering her the delights of her heart.

"Just so you know, I've made another

decision tonight. This place where we are standing has been home to six generations of my family. The Turners belong here, Amanda. I want to raise my children—our children—here on Turner land. I'm going to open a small law office in town where I can practice and also do some consulting work for my firm. *And* I thought, if you do fall in love with me and become my wife, that you could head up a pro bono division working to get amputees the therapy they need for the time that they need it."

Amanda felt a trail of tears spill out of her eyes. He'd thought of all of this. "Oh, Wyatt. You make it all seem so easy."

He smiled that crooked, wonderful, curl-her-toes smile. "All you have to do is say that you love me."

Amanda's heart felt like it might burst. She hesitated for a moment, inhaled deeply and then wrapped her arms around his neck. She couldn't stop herself. For a woman who'd had to fight for every step forward since she was fourteen, all the fight drained from her and she simply did and said what was in her heart…. "I love you."

Wyatt closed his eyes and lifted his face

toward heaven. "Thank you, God. Thank you." And then he kissed her.

And Amanda felt God's smile and it filled every dark spot inside of her with hope and light, and she felt whole.

It was the most wonderful feeling she'd ever experienced.

Epilogue

"You boys want a barbecue plate?" Applegate asked, waving a sausage link from behind a long table that he, Sam and Stanley were manning.

Wyatt stood in the yard of the stagecoach house, where tents had been set up for his wedding to Amanda. They'd thrown a regular party to celebrate. Across the way, he caught Amanda smiling at him. She looked beautiful in her white dress, and to him she was the most radiant woman God had ever created. There was no other like her.

"Save one for me, will you?" he said, inching toward her.

"Will do. Chance, how 'bout you?"

"Thanks, App. I'd appreciate it if you'd store a plate back for me, too."

App's bushy brows crinkled like a caterpillar inching across the floor. "You ever thank about movin' home, Chance? That rodeo'ns got ta be gettin' old. We need a good preacher. Jest ask Wyatt, he knows what kind a lazy preachin' we been hearin' since Pastor Allen had ta retar."

Chance grimaced. "I'm sorry y'all are havin' a hard time, sir. But until the good Lord brings me back, I'll be out there on the circuit. I'll keep praying that the Lord sends the right man to y'all. He's got him out there, you can be assured of that. It'll just be in His timing that he gets here. Be patient and give the ones that come a prayerful consideration."

App grunted, fiddling with his hearing aid. "It ain't as easy as you thank."

Wyatt felt for the town. He knew Applegate wanted what was best for the town. He was grumpy because he missed Pastor Allen, who'd been there for a while but had to leave when his wife became ill and needed to be closer to the doctors who were taking care of her. Change was hard. While he wasn't sure if all the pastors who'd come in were as bad as the one that he'd heard that first Sunday he'd gone to church, they hadn't been right, either. "When the right man shows up, God will lead y'all and you'll know," he offered, and Chance agreed. Honestly, he'd like it if Chance felt called to Mule Hollow, but Wyatt didn't see that happening anytime soon. Chance *was* doing what he was called to do.

Stanley, who'd been busy cutting up brisket on the table behind App, brought a new trayful to App's table. "The question is will we survive till he gets here!" Stanley boomed over the music.

"You'll survive," Wyatt said, distracted by his bride as she started his way.

"God's timing is perfect, I'm proof of that," he said. He left the others to their discussion and met Amanda in the center of the tent. She walked into his open arms. "Have I told you how blessed I feel today?" he asked, kissing her temple and holding her tightly.

"Me, too," she whispered against his ear. "God is good, isn't He?"

Wyatt leaned his head back, feeling

humbled by God's goodness. "God is great. He sent me you, and I can't wait to see the plans He has for us as a family."

* * * * *

Watch for Debra Clopton's next
Steeple Hill Love Inspired
YUKON COWBOY.
Part of the ALASKAN BRIDE RUSH
continuity miniseries
On sale September 28, 2010 and
Chance's story, YULETIDE COWBOY, in
the MEN OF MULE HOLLOW *miniseries*
On sale November 23, 2010

Dear Reader,

As always, I'm thrilled when you decide to spend time with me and the gang in Mule Hollow! Thank you so much for letting me entertain you for a few hours. I've loved coming up with all the different men in the MEN OF MULE HOLLOW series, and I knew when I introduced the Turner men in the first book, *Lone Star Cinderella*, that I was going to have fun telling their stories. Creating Wyatt was a challenge, and I couldn't wait to write his story.

You see, I'm a bit like Wyatt when it comes to being an overachiever…and being stubborn. I think I'm Superwoman and I hold myself up to an unrealistic level just as Wyatt sort of thought he was a superman. God had to show me this past year that sometimes I can rely on myself too much when what I need to do is rely on Him. I wanted to create a character who had to be taught this same lesson, and so I took Wyatt out of his comfort zone and threw him into uncharted waters when he found himself helpless. God says that when we are weak He is strong. I have found this is true, and Wyatt also found this is true. If you are trying to handle too much by yourself I pray that you will reevaluate, relax and let God help you and give you strength. He is waiting. And in doing this you will give Him the glory He deserves since it is He and not ourselves who deserves our high praise!

I love to hear from readers! You can reach me at P.O. Box 1125, Madisonville, Texas, or debraclopton.com. I hope until I see you again that you live, laugh and do give God the glory.

P.S. I have a book in the fun new ALASKAN BRIDE RUSH continuity, *Yukon Cowboy*, coming out in October, and then watch for the last of the MEN OF MULE HOLLOW series, *Yuletide Cowboy*, coming in December. Chance, the rodeo preacher, comes home to Mule Hollow. He meets a resident of the local women's shelter and her twin boys as they move into their own place just in time for Christmas.

QUESTIONS FOR DISCUSSION

1 Did you enjoy this story? If so, what aspect drew you to it?

2 Wyatt is an overachiever. Do you know someone in your life who is this way or are you this way yourself? Discuss the good aspects or drawbacks that you see.

3 Amanda shows real courage in the way she accepts the loss of her leg. Her father was the person who helped her realize she still had things to be thankful for, which helped her move forward with her life. Do you know someone who has done this?

4 It is through her disability that Amanda realizes her purpose in life. What is her purpose?

5 There are many people who have lived through tragedy, heartache and other problems to realize that they can use their experience to help others. Have you done this or do you know someone who has done this?

6 How have they touched your life or those around them?

7 Do you believe that God puts people in your life when you need them? How has He done this?

8 God says He will make good from bad situations for those who love him. I personally have seen Him do this in my own life over and over again. Can you give your testimony to the readers' group about how He has done this in your life?

9 Wyatt is really hard on himself. Why is that? What lessons did he need to learn?

10 In 2 *Corinthians* 12:10, it says, "Therefore I take pleasure in infirmities, in reproaches, in necessities, in persecutions, in distresses for Christ's sake: for when I am weak, then am I strong." I love this verse from Paul. It is so wonderfully true if we think about it. When we are weak then we are strong because we must rely on Christ's strength. I have to remind

myself of this almost daily when I begin to worry about something. How did Wyatt have to learn this?

11 The prior verse, 2 *Corinthians* 12:8-9, explains it: "For this thing I besought the Lord thrice, that it might depart from me. And He said unto me, My grace is sufficient for thee: for my strength is made perfect in weakness." How did both Wyatt and Amanda learn this?

12 The last of the verse Paul says, "Most gladly therefore will I rather glory in my infirmities, that the power of Christ may rest upon me." When Amanda lost her leg, she found the strength of these verses and used her life as a testament to God, letting Him rest upon her, and use her. Do you think she will be able to use her inability to have children as a witness for God in the years ahead of her? How can she do this?

13 Amanda says she feels worthless and empty. Chance tells Wyatt to help her know that the emptiness she is feeling

could be filled with God's grace if she would let it. God is the ultimate comforter and loves her and wants only the best for her. He also tells Wyatt that God would use Amanda's situation for good if she would let him. That promise is in *Romans* 8:28. "And we know that all things work together for good to them that love God, to them who are the called according to His purpose." Do you believe this is true? Can you see how God can fill any emptiness or sorrow that we might have and help us to help others in similar situations? Discuss this with the others in the group.

14 Amanda and Wyatt are really strong people. As a couple, how do you think they can touch lives and be a team for God?

Love™ Inspired® SUSPENSE

RIVETING INSPIRATIONAL ROMANCE

Watch for our new series of
edge-of-your-seat suspense novels.
These contemporary tales
of intrigue and romance
feature Christian characters
facing challenges to their faith...
and their lives!

NOW AVAILABLE IN REGULAR
& LARGER-PRINT FORMATS

Steeple
Hill®

Visit:
www.SteepleHill.com

Love Inspired.
HISTORICAL

INSPIRATIONAL HISTORICAL ROMANCE

Engaging stories of romance,
adventure and faith,
these novels are set in
various historical periods
from biblical times
to World War II.

NOW AVAILABLE!

**Steeple
Hill®**